Life, Loss, and Lemonade

Saturday, April 18, 8:42 a.m.

Two days before my 15th birthday

My birthday plans went up in smoke. Literally.

Last night, while the good citizens of Faraway, Alabama, slept, the paint-your-own pottery place in downtown Faraway where I was supposed to be having my birthday party today burned to the ground. I know this because Dad got me out of bed to see the morning news segment about it. I wasn't the only one he woke. I hobbled down the hall on my crutches behind the rest of my family as we all went to watch the report.

"Look, Mom! There's your store," May pointed to the TV, and there was Tibra's Fashions in the background. Mom's store is down the street from Clay Makers, and it was pretty unsettling, especially to Mom, to see that it was in such close proximity to a business that was now in ashes.

"What do you think caused the fire?" Mom asked Dad, after the reporter said the source of the blaze was still under investigation.

"It could be anything," Dad said. "Faulty wiring could do it."

"Or arson," said June.

Mom, Dad, and I all looked at my little sister. Surprisingly, she's only in third grade. Intellectually, that's a different picture.

"What's arson?" asked May.

"When you burn something down on purpose, usually for insurance money," June explained.

May winced. "I don't know if it was arson, but it's terrible. Clay Makers was special. I hate to think that there's someone who

THE MOSTLY MISERABLE LIFE OF APRIL SINCLAIR

Life, Loss, and Lemonade

LAURIE FRIEDMAN

MINNEAPOLIS

Darby Creek
A division of Lerner Publishing Group, Inc.
241 First Avenue North
Minneapolis, MN 55401 USA

For reading levels and more information, look up this title at www.lernerbooks.com.

Main body text set in Janson Text LT Std 12/17.
Typeface provided by Linotype AG.

Library of Congress Cataloging-in-Publication Data

The Cataloging-in-Publication Data for *Life, Loss, and Lemonade* is on file at the Library of Congress.
ISBN 978-1-4677-8591-4 (hardcover)
ISBN 978-1-5124-2699-1 (EB pdf)

Manufactured in the United States of America
1-37944-19402-9/27/2016

For my Alabama Family—
Uncle Harold, Kit, Lisa, and in loving
memory, Aunt Joanie and Bo.
With all my love,
L.B.F.

Before the sun sets on her sixteenth birthday, she will prick her finger on the spindle of a spinning wheel, and fall into a sleep like death!

—*Maleficent*

Saturday, April 18, 8:42 a.m.
Two days before my 15th birthday

My birthday plans went up in smoke. Literally.

Last night, while the good citizens of Faraway, Alabama, slept, the paint-your-own pottery place in downtown Faraway where I was supposed to be having my birthday party today burned to the ground. I know this because Dad got me out of bed to see the morning news segment about it. I wasn't the only one he woke. I hobbled down the hall on my crutches behind the rest of my family as

1

we all went to watch the report.

"Look, Mom! There's your store!" May pointed to the TV, and there was Flora's Fashions in the background. Mom's store is down the street from Clay Makers, and it was pretty unsettling, especially for Mom, to see that it was in such close proximity to a business that was now in ashes.

"What do you think caused the fire?" Mom asked Dad, after the reporter said the source of the blaze was still under investigation.

"It could be anything," Dad said. "Faulty wiring. A bad kiln."

"Or arson," said June.

Mom, Dad, and I all looked at my little sister. Chronologically, she's nine and in third grade. Intellectually—that's a different story.

"What's arson?" asked May.

"When you burn something down on purpose, usually to get money," June explained.

May winced. I wasn't sure if it was because the idea of committing arson was repugnant to her, or the fact that she's in middle school and didn't like being given a vocab lesson by her younger sister.

"How do you know about arson?" Mom asked June.

"I read a book about a kid whose dad burned down his family grocery store to collect the insurance proceeds. He didn't get them because what he did was a crime. He ended up in prison and the kid had to go live with his aunt."

Mom gave Dad a look of disapproval. "I think we might need to monitor what she's reading."

"That's censorship," responded June.

"Excuse me," I said, signaling a time-out. "I think the more important issue we need to be discussing is what I'm going to do for my birthday."

While I was feeling sympathetic toward June, who clearly had no desire to have her reading choices examined, and awful for the owners of Clay Makers, who just had their business burn down, I was feeling bad for myself too. I was supposed to be celebrating my fifteenth birthday this afternoon with all of my friends at a place that no longer existed.

I looked at Mom and Dad, waiting to hear their suggestions, but they just shook their heads like they didn't have any other ideas. To be fair, this wasn't the first time we'd had to rethink my party plans. Originally, I was going to have a skating party. That might sound kind of lame, and it would be if you lived in a place like New York, Los Angeles, or even Omaha, Nebraska. But when you live in Faraway, Alabama, it's not like there's a plethora of party venues. I was actually excited to have my party at Wheels Up. But when we went snow skiing over spring break with Gaga and Willy and the rest of my family, I fell and broke my leg. I couldn't exactly skate with my leg in a cast.

When my plans fell through, I wasn't the only one who was upset. May and June, the girls on the dance team, and especially Sophie and Billy were disappointed.

"This was a big deal for me," said Sophie. "I'm moving back to New York at the end of the school year, and this was probably my only opportunity to experience that slice of small-town America."

"Trust me, skating rinks aren't that great," I told her.

But she was disappointed, and so was Billy. I've seen him show off his moves on wheels more times than I can count, but this was going to be the first time Sophie would see him skate, and he couldn't wait to impress his girlfriend.

When it became clear that skating wasn't an option, Mom suggested I have a painting party at Clay Makers, and the rest is history.

Honestly, I'm not surprised my plans fell through again.

"I'm birthday-cursed," I said to my parents.

"April, don't be ridiculous," said Dad.

"Hear me out," I said, determined to make my point. "At six, Mom was pregnant with June and on bed rest. When I turned seven, I had strep throat." I paused and pointed to Dad. "At eight, you dropped the cupcakes you brought to my class. My ninth backyard birthday party was rained out. At ten, one of the girls at my sleepover party had lice and everyone else got them."

I paused as I thought about my eleventh and twelfth birthdays. I had a cooking party and a scavenger hunt, which my former BFF Brynn helped plan. Ironically, those were the only parties that turned out well. But that phase of good birthday karma was short-lived.

When I turned thirteen, my parents planned the unfortunate and unforgettable *Spring Has Sprung* party for my sisters and me, when June practically announced to everyone at the party that I had a crush on Matt Parker, who had just moved in next door. Then, at fourteen, when I was actually going out with Matt, I spent my birthday waiting around for him to show up and celebrate with me. When he finally did, it was late at night and he tried to feel me up on my own front porch. It was a complete disaster.

Those weren't memories I wanted to relive with my family. "I've had a lot of bad birthdays," I said. "And this year is clearly falling into that category." I shrugged. "It must be a curse."

"April, it's silly to be afraid there's some kind

of birthday curse." Mom looked me in the eye. "Fear has never been anyone's friend."

I had to laugh.

"I'm not afraid I'm cursed," I told her. "I'm convinced of it."

Sunday, April 19, 9:45 p.m.
Last day of being fourteen

It has been decided. For my birthday, I'm going to eat dinner with my family.

It doesn't feel like much of a celebration since I would have done that anyway, but a.) I know from experience I'm better off not planning something that wouldn't have worked out, and b.) now that I know this is probably the last birthday I'll get to spend with Gaga, having dinner with my family doesn't sound so bad.

I get why Gaga chose not to have surgery or chemotherapy or radiation. She's old, she has terminal cancer, and she doesn't want to go through the side effects, which sound awful. Still, it doesn't make me happy knowing that one day soon Gaga will die. I've thought about it plenty, and it's not something I wanted to think about on the day before I turned fifteen. So instead, I called Sophie. "We're all going for dinner tomorrow night to celebrate my birthday," I told her.

Sophie clucked her tongue. "I know," she said sympathetically.

Her tone irritated me. "I'm cool with it," I said.

"Well, I'm coming over today and we're having a pre-birthday celebration."

I get why she offered. When her grandfather married Gaga, Sophie and I became almost-cousins. Then, when Sophie's parents split up and she and her mom, Emma, moved to Faraway to live with Willy and Gaga, Sophie and I developed an unspoken pact that we'd always have each other's backs. But it annoyed me when she volunteered to come over to celebrate, because I felt like a birthday charity case. I would have liked it more if she'd just acknowledged that in her view, my birthday was a bust. When she got to my house, her upbeat mood was really getting on my nerves.

"Tomorrow is your birthday!" Her voice was high-pitched like she was singing, not talking. "So what do you want to do today?"

I stuck my casted leg in her face. "Zumba."

Sophie rolled her eyes. "April, you only turn fifteen once. I have a great idea for how we can celebrate."

I couldn't imagine what she had in mind. As it turned out, we spent the day sitting on my bed and going through my old pictures on my computer. It would have been fun, except that May and June came into my room while we were doing it and wanted to know if they could look too. I said *no* at the same time that Sophie said *yes*.

"They can stay," Sophie said. She patted the space on the bed between us, and May and June plopped down without waiting for my permission. I love my sisters, but when Sophie let them join us, I knew the pictures they'd want to look at were the ones of themselves.

May practically hijacked my laptop from me and kept scrolling to all of the pictures of her when she was little. "Look, that's me diving into the pool, and me hitting a softball, and me playing Frisbee with Gilligan."

"You were adorable," said Sophie as she looked at the pictures.

Then June wanted a turn. She took the computer from May and scrolled to the pictures I had of her when she was learning to walk. "I was a darling baby," she told Sophie.

"You sure were." Sophie leaned over and looked at the screen. Then she turned the laptop toward me. "Look how cute she was, April."

I looked, but I'd seen those pictures of my sisters dozens of times.

When they finally left my room, Sophie said, "They're so cute."

"I see them every day," I said. "Their cuteness is less of a novelty to me."

Sophie recoiled. "You're so lucky you have sisters. I wish I did."

I was going to let her comment slide. I'm sure it's hard being an only child, especially right now, with her parents going through a divorce. But then she added, "You should be nicer to May and June."

"I'm really nice to May and June," I said defensively.

Sophie nodded like that was true, at least partially. "I'm just saying that sometimes you get impatient with them."

I felt my anger rising. "Don't you think you're being kind of judgmental? Particularly when we're supposed to be celebrating my birthday."

Sophie looked down and picked at a rip in the leg of her jeans. "When you're right, you're right," she said. "I'm sorry."

I could tell she genuinely was. "No worries." I bumped my shoulder into hers. "You're going back to New York in five weeks. The last thing we need to do is get into an argument."

Sophie laughed. "Like that would happen." She linked her arm through mine. "One of my favorite things about being friends with you is that we never fight."

"Yeah," I said. She was right. In the year Sophie lived in Faraway, we always got along. From time to time, like today, one of us might have said something that annoyed the other person, but it was never a big deal. We'd never had a real fight, which made my friendship with her the polar opposite of my friendship with Brynn. Brynn and I had been best friends since kindergarten, but we spent the whole last year fighting, and now we're not friends at all.

As I thought about Brynn, it made me realize how lucky I've been to have Sophie here this year and how much I'm going to miss her. "I'm sorry I've been grumpy today," I said to Sophie.

"I'm going to miss you too," Sophie said, like she could read my mind. She pretend-pouted, so I did too. Then we both cracked up.

If you have to fight with somebody, that's the way to do it.

10:02 p.m.

Dad just came into my room to remind me that tomorrow I turn fifteen, and that after school we have an appointment at the Alabama Department of Public Safety so I can get my driver's permit. I can't wait! The Driver's Ed course Dad signed me up for doesn't start until I get my cast off, but as soon as I pass the written exam, at least I'll have my permit. I guess that's a big assumption. Though I'm certain I'll fall within the range of Alabamians who've passed this test, it's possible my bad birthday luck could somehow strike. I don't want to jinx myself, but I know the manual cold.

So I have to ask: what could possibly go wrong?

I think I'm afraid to be happy

because whenever I get too happy,

something bad always happens.

—*Charlie Brown*

Monday, April 20, 7:15 a.m.
Happy birthday to me!

My fifteenth birthday is off to a surprisingly great start. Leo called from college and woke me up with the birthday song. He said he set his alarm so he'd be the first person to serenade me. It meant a lot, since I don't think of college students as people who like to get up early and sing.

At breakfast, May and June gave me handmade cards. Mom made birthday pancakes and put a candle in my stack. Dad had to leave for the diner early, but he promised he'd pick me up from school and we'd go straight to the DPS before dinner with Gaga and the rest of my family.

Even the weather is cooperating. There's no humidity, so I have straight, frizz-free hair.

So far, so good!

1:17 p.m.
Study Hall

My day continues to go shockingly well.

Sophie and Billy were waiting for me at my locker this morning with cupcakes Sophie made. In homeroom, Mrs. Monteleone had everyone sing "Happy Birthday." At lunch, my cousin Harry got my tray without asking, which meant I didn't have to hobble through the lunch line looking for help like I've been doing since I came back to school on crutches after spring break.

And while we waited for English class to start, I even had a pleasant conversation with Billy when he brought up a controversial topic.

"You're going to have a double celebration

this year," he said. Billy reminded me I get to celebrate my birthday on birthday night at camp this summer. Then he grinned. "Just one of the many perks you have to look forward to as one of the oldest campers."

I figured my birthday was the perfect opportunity to tell Billy something he didn't want to hear. "I'm not going back to camp."

Billy looked unpleasantly surprised. "You have to go back," he said. "It's our last summer."

I didn't think I should have to remind Billy that the previous summer at camp wasn't so great for me. What would I have said?

Hey Billy, remember how you, Brynn, and I became best friends in third grade, and then you and Brynn started going out last summer and neither of you bothered to tell me? Well, that sort of ruined camp, which is why I'm not going back. Oh, and then you broke up with Brynn and now she's not speaking to you, or to me for that matter. So I don't see either of us going back. But have fun!

It didn't seem like that was the thing to say to Billy, especially when he'd brought me cupcakes this morning.

"I know what you're thinking," said Billy, like he could read my mind. "We can't change what happened. But it doesn't mean we can't have a good summer this year."

Fortunately, the bell rang then and class started, which meant I didn't have to tell Billy I didn't want to spend my birthday talking about something I had no intention of doing. I think he got it anyway.

"Just enjoy your birthday," he mouthed.

Maybe the birthday gods are with me after all.

4:54 p.m.
Cursed!

My birthday curse is real and so much worse than I ever knew it could be. When the last bell rang, I went to meet Dad on the south side of school where he'd planned to pick me up, so we could go to the DPS. But as soon as I got my crutches and myself into the car, I could tell something was wrong.

"April, there's been a change of plans," he said. His tone was so serious it scared me. "Gaga had to go to the hospital," said Dad. "She was having trouble breathing this morning, so Willy took her. Your mom, Aunt Lilly, and Aunt Lila are there with her."

I felt tears forming. "Is she going to be OK?"

"We're going to go pick up May and June," Dad said, which didn't answer my question, so I repeated it. "I don't know," Dad said honestly. "The hospital is running some tests, and we're going to have to wait to find out."

I nodded. But as we drove to the middle school to get May and then to the elementary school for June, I felt fear creeping up inside me like a fast-growing ivy vine in a cartoon. The feeling started in my gut and made its way up my esophagus and into my throat. By the time we got home, I felt like the fear had crept into every corner of my body. I called Sophie and Harry to see if they had heard what was going on and if they knew more than I did.

The only thing I found out is that they're just as worried as I am.

9:14 p.m.
Home from dinner

By dinnertime, Mom was still at the hospital, so Dad took May, June, Sophie, and me out to celebrate my birthday. Honestly, I didn't even want to go. I wasn't hungry, but Dad said we had to eat. We went to Mamma Mia, my favorite pizza place in Faraway, and I still had to force myself to eat a slice. When the server brought out a piece of cake with the candle in it, I closed my eyes and made a wish that Gaga will be OK.

It's funny—though not in a ha-ha way—the difference a day can make. Yesterday, I thought it sounded lame to be celebrating my fifteenth birthday at a family dinner.

Tonight, I couldn't think of anything I'd rather be doing.

10:02 p.m.

Mom just called to tell me good night. "April, I'm so sorry we couldn't all be together for your birthday." Her voice sounded tired.

"How's Gaga?" I asked.

"She's sleeping now," said Mom. "We'll know more in the next few days."

"Are you coming home tonight?" I asked.

"I'm here with Aunt Lila and Aunt Lilly. At least one of us will stay at the hospital tonight. Emma took Willy home. He was exhausted."

As hard as this was for everyone, I could only imagine how Willy must be feeling. It's bad enough that Gaga is sick, but I'm sure he's also thinking about the fact that Emma and Sophie are moving back to New York when Sophie is done with school. "How's Willy doing?"

"That's sweet of you to ask," said Mom. She paused. "He's having a hard time with all of this."

When she said that, a feeling of guilt swept over me. "Mom, do you think I'm being punished for all that stuff I said about my birthday being cursed?"

"April, Gaga has cancer. Her being in the hospital has nothing to do with anything you did or said."

Hopefully, Mom is right. But when I hung

up the phone, I closed my eyes. I'd already made my birthday wish at Mamma Mia, but I said a prayer that Gaga will be OK.

I sincerely hope birthday prayers get special consideration.

Why, sometimes I've believed as many as six impossible things before breakfast.

—*Lewis Carroll*, Through the Looking-Glass

Wednesday, April 22, 8:22 p.m.
At home

Tonight, Mom was at the hospital and Dad was at the diner. They asked me if I'd stay home with May and June. All I was supposed to be doing was babysitting and making dinner, not answering tough questions. But I ended up doing that too.

"Is Gaga going to die?" May asked when we sat down to eat turkey sandwiches and tomato soup. I choked on a bite of soup.

"Everyone dies," said June matter-of-factly.

I looked at May, who was getting teary-eyed. June wasn't wrong, but her answer clearly wasn't what May needed to hear.

"Gaga has a collapsed lung," I said, choosing my words carefully.

June wasn't as cautious. "Mom said she's having difficulty breathing and eating, and that she has other complications."

When Mom came home from the hospital last night, she'd updated me on Gaga's condition. I heard her having a similar conversation with June this morning.

As May wiped her eyes with her napkin, I realized she wasn't ready to hear any of it yet. Even though she's almost twelve, she seemed so small and sad as she sat there crying. I just wanted her to feel better. I put my spoon down and reached over and squeezed her hand. "We should all stay positive," I said.

May looked at me like I should keep going with my words of encouragement. But honestly, I didn't know what else to say. It was making me uncomfortable, so I was glad when June told me she found a hair in her sandwich.

I stood up, dumped her sandwich in the trash, and got the turkey back out of the refrigerator.

It's a lot easier to fix a new sandwich than a broken heart.

10:17 p.m.
Talked with Dad

Tonight May and June had already gone to bed and Mom was still at the hospital. I couldn't sleep, so I went into Dad's room. "Can we talk?" I asked.

Dad was in bed watching TV. He picked up the remote and hit Mute. Then he patted the spot on the bed next to him and smiled like he was glad I was there. I hobbled over and settled in on the bed. "What's on your mind?" he asked.

I hadn't been sure what I was going to say, but when I opened my mouth, nothing came out. My inability to express what I was thinking made me emotional. Dad saw it. He handed me a tissue and then wrapped an arm around me. I rested my head on the front of his shoulder. It felt good to be there.

"I know you're worried about Gaga. We all are," he said.

I told him about my conversation with May and June about staying positive. "That was a very mature thing you told your sisters," said Dad.

"Do you think it helps to stay positive?" I asked.

Dad gave me a long look before he answered my question. It was the gentle look he used to give me when I was little if I'd gotten injured or if something didn't go my way. "It can't hurt," he said.

Thursday, April 23, 7:04 p.m.
Home from Harry's

I want to stay positive, like I'd told May we should, but Gaga's condition has taken a turn for the worse. Or so I hear.

This afternoon, Ms. Baumann said she didn't need me at dance practice. I've been her "helper" since I broke my leg, but the truth is that she's so capable that it's mostly been a title with no duties. I think I've only helped her twice. Since I didn't have to stay, I ended up going with Sophie over to Harry and Amanda's house to hang out.

We decided to go there because we knew it was where we'd get the most information. Aunt Lilly has become the self-appointed contact person between the doctors and Gaga. I don't know if it's because she's older than my mom and Aunt Lila, or if it's just because she has an insatiable need to always be the one in charge. Either way, she always seems to be the first one to know what's going on.

And today was no exception. We were all hanging out in Amanda's room when we overheard Aunt Lilly on the phone. "I'm the oldest of three sisters, so my mother's care has fallen to me," we heard her tell whomever she was talking to.

Honestly, I think my mom or Aunt Lila would have been happy for Gaga's care to "fall to" them. The problem was that Aunt Lilly would never allow that to happen.

I wanted to say something, but who would I say something to?

There was no point telling Harry and Amanda. They'd just agree. They hate how bossy their mom is. Plus, I wanted to hear what else Aunt Lilly was saying. She was talking about "end-of-life care." It was a new term for me, and apparently for Sophie, Harry, and Amanda too. We all strained to hear exactly what she was saying.

"*End of life* is a nice way of saying death," Harry said when Aunt Lilly finished her call.

"Shut up." Amanda punched Harry in the arm.

"Just because she used the term, that doesn't mean Gaga is dying right away," said Sophie. "It means she's nearing the end, which could be tomorrow or next week or next month." Sophie nodded as she spoke, like she was convincing herself. "You don't know how long it will be," she added. "It could even be next year."

"It's going to be sooner rather than later," said Harry. "She's been in the hospital since Monday."

"A girl in my grade, Deidre Davis, was in the hospital a week when she had her appendix out," said Amanda.

Harry rolled his eyes at his sister. "Deidre Davis is in middle school and she had an infection. She's not eighty years old and diagnosed with terminal cancer."

"I read that you can cure cancer by drinking wheatgrass juice," said Sophie. She sounded hopeful.

Harry laughed. "Gaga has spent a lifetime eating fried chicken and ham sandwiches. I don't see her switching to wheatgrass juice now."

Gaga has tried to eat healthier in the last few years, but I kind of agreed with Harry.

"I'm going to suggest it to her," said Sophie. "She might do it."

"Yeah," said Amanda, who seemed to be on Team Sophie. "She's right. Gaga has a lot to live for. Kids. Grandkids. A husband." She squinted her eyes at her brother. "You're so negative."

Harry looked shocked. "Since when did you become the voice of positivity?"

He had a point. After Harry, Amanda is the most negative person I know. Still, even though she wears tons of makeup, has boobs bigger than mine, and definitely acts like she's in high school, she's only a year older than May. It was easy to see she was just as sad and scared as my sister.

"We all need to stay positive," I said, repeating the message I'd given May and June. But as I looked around the room, everyone there seemed to be thinking the same thing— that our attitude might not make a difference.

Friday, April 24, 10:02 p.m.
Talked to Leo

"I can't wait to come home," Leo said when I answered the phone. Then he launched into an explanation of college final exams and how hard they're supposed to be.

Usually I enjoy hearing what he has to say when he talks about college. It feels like a glimpse into the future. But tonight when he called, my mind was elsewhere. "I'm sure you'll do well," I said absentmindedly.

After he finished talking about his study plans, he switched topics to the summer ahead. "It'll be fun to hang out," he said. I agreed, but I zoned out as he talked about getting his old job back at the deli when he comes home. I had much more important things to think about than ham and turkey.

"Earth to April," said Leo. "You're so distracted. What's up?"

I hadn't planned to talk about Gaga's condition with him. I wasn't ready to share it with anyone, to make it more real that way, but it all spilled out. Leo listened quietly until I was done.

"I'm sorry to hear that. It sounds serious."

Leo isn't a doctor, but he's a seventeen-year-old science genius, so I thought he might know the answer to a question I had. "What happens as a body starts to shut down?" I paused. I'd been thinking about this since yesterday, when I'd overheard Aunt Lilly's end-of-life-conversation. I didn't want to ask the next part of my question, but I needed to. "You know, like, how long does it take?"

"To die?" Leo asked gently.

"Yeah," I stammered. My voice was barely a whisper.

"Well, every body is different. But once a body has trouble breathing and eating, it's just a matter of days, maybe a week or so, before vital organs cease to work."

"That's not what I wanted to hear," I said. I knew my voice tone was too sharp.

Leo paused like he was thinking of what he could say that would make me feel better. "Gaga is a fighter."

That was true, but I wasn't sure if it was enough. I had another question for Leo. "Do you believe in God?" I asked. In all our talks, it wasn't something we'd discussed.

"Well, I think there's more to life than organs, cells, and particles," said Leo. "But I've always kind of questioned the existence of a God."

He paused.

"April, are you OK?" Leo asked.

"I don't really want to talk about this anymore," I said.

Leo said he understood, but as we hung up, I wasn't sure he did.

10:17 p.m.
Talked to Leo
Again

After we hung up, Leo called back. "I'm sorry if I upset you," he said. "Just because I don't believe in something doesn't mean you have to feel the same way."

"I know," I said defensively.

"It also doesn't mean I'm right."

"Thanks," I said. Then there was a long pause like neither of us knew what to say.

"Want to hear a joke?" Leo finally asked.

"Definitely," I said.

"It's dirty."

"I like dirty jokes," I told him.

Leo cleared his throat. "What did the dirt say when it began to rain?"

"What?" I asked.

"If this keeps up, my name will be mud."

It was so corny, but I had to laugh.

"I'm a fountain of dirty jokes," said Leo. "But I like to save them for when someone needs cheering up. I find it makes them feel better."

Oddly enough, he was right.

It's important to tell the people you love how much you love them while they can hear you.

—*Meredith Grey*

Sunday, April 26, 9:18 p.m.
Home from Gaga and Willy's house

The good news is that Gaga came home from the hospital. No one said why she got to come home. Part of me wonders if it's because there was nothing else the hospital could do to help her, or if it's just because Mom, Aunt Lilly, and Aunt Lila thought she'd be more comfortable in her own environment.

Either way, I was glad and everyone else was too.

The first thing I did when I heard she was

home was call Sophie. One of the best things about Sophie and Emma living with Willy and Gaga is that Sophie can be my eyes and ears on the ground. "How does Gaga seem to you?" I asked.

"Happy to be here. But my grandpa got kind of upset when she got home."

I frowned. "I would have thought he would have been happier than anyone."

"In a way, he was," said Sophie. "We hung a *Welcome Home* banner for her, and he did a little happy dance when he saw her, which made her smile."

That was a nice mental image to have. "So what was the problem?"

"Aunt Lilly," said Sophie. She paused, letting her words sink in. After that day that we'd been at Harry and Amanda's, Sophie and I had discussed what we heard Aunt Lilly say about being the one in charge, and neither of us liked it.

Sophie continued to explain what happened. "When Gaga came home from the hospital, Aunt Lilly was at the house. My grandpa was trying to help Gaga get into bed, and Aunt Lilly told him she'd do it." Sophie paused. "He let her do it and he was nice about it, but it upset him. It was like telling him he wasn't needed."

I grunted into the phone. "That's awful."

"Yeah."

When Sophie and I hung up, she promised to call and text throughout the day, giving me updates on Gaga's condition, which she did. Gaga sat up in bed. Gaga took a nap. Gaga took a sip of water. A nurse came to stay with Gaga. Gaga took her medicine. Gaga took another nap.

I appreciated being kept in the loop, but I was anxious to see Gaga myself. I know everyone else was too, which I think is why Mom and my aunts decided we would all go over there for dinner tonight.

I was glad I got to see her, but the night was pretty different from any other night we've ever had at Gaga's. And it wasn't just because Gaga was in her room with a nurse, or that my mom and her sisters kept taking turns at her bedside, while the rest of us congregated without her. When my family sat down to eat dinner, there was this lull, like no one knew what to say. My family is always so talkative and opinionated, but there was a long silent stretch where everyone just sat there eating without saying a word.

Finally, Izzy broke the silence. "Are we playing the Quiet Game?" she asked.

"You lose," said Charlotte, pointing her finger at Izzy.

Izzy crossed her arms across her chest. "I don't care. I hate that game."

"We're not playing a game," said June. "Everyone is quiet because no one knows what to say."

"How come?" asked Izzy.

"June." Mom gave her a look like she wanted to stop her from saying whatever was about to come next. But it didn't work.

June turned toward Izzy. "Because Gaga is sick and that's what everyone is thinking about, so it's hard to talk about other stuff."

"Is it the cancer?" asked Izzy.

Izzy and Charlotte knew Gaga had cancer,

but I don't think they really knew what it meant. Mom gave Aunt Lila a look that said she was sorry June had opened up a dialogue she might not be ready to have with her six-year-old daughters. "Why don't we eat dessert now," said Mom, who clearly wanted to stop the conversation from going any further. "When we're done, you kids can all take turns going in to see Gaga." She started to slice the chocolate cake Aunt Lila had made, and she passed around plates.

Her strategy seemed to work, because both Izzy and Charlotte turned their attention from cancer to cake.

I ate my slice and thought about what I was going to say to Gaga when it was my turn. But as soon as I saw her, I forgot the dialogue I'd rehearsed in my head. I hadn't been allowed to visit Gaga at the hospital, so it had been over a week since I'd seen her, and I was shocked by how much her condition had worsened. She looked older and much more frail. Her skin was a yellowish color and she had bruises on her arms and face.

"You look like you got in a fight," I said as I sat down in the chair beside her bed.

I hoped even in her state she would appreciate my humor. But she didn't respond. "Is she asleep?" I asked the nurse.

"Not quite yet," said the nurse. "But she took her meds a few minutes ago. They help with the pain, but she's a little out of it."

I didn't want Gaga to be in pain, but I also didn't want her to be out of it. As I sat beside her, my brain flooded with things I needed to say to her. "Gaga, please get better," I finally said. "I love you and I have some important things I want to talk to you about."

I know Gaga loves nothing more than talking about important things so I thought for sure that would get her to react, but she didn't respond. I felt panic rising in me that she might not ever respond. I picked up her hand and squeezed it lightly. "Gaga, please just give me a sign you know I'm here," I said.

Gaga squeezed my hand, such a light squeeze I almost wasn't sure she'd done it on purpose. Yet I knew she had. Relief flooded through me that Gaga was still Gaga. But now that I'm home and I've had time to think about it, I have to say I'm as mildly and temporarily relieved as a human can be.

I keep thinking about the conversations I've had lately with May and June and Dad, Harry and Amanda, and Sophie, and even Leo about the power of positive thinking.

I know it's important to think positively.

But after what I saw tonight, it's kind of hard to do.

Science, my lad, is made up of mistakes, but they are mistakes which it is useful to make, because they lead little by little to the truth.

—*Jules Verne*, Journey to the Center of the Earth

Tuesday, April 28, 7:02 p.m.
Back at Gaga's house

What a difference forty-eight hours can make.

I'm happy (and shocked!) to report that Gaga made a turnaround. It's so weird. Sunday night she couldn't even talk, and today she sat up in bed. I found this out when Sophie texted me while I was at dance practice.

Sophie: Home from school.
Sophie: Gaga sitting up in bed talking to my grandpa!

Sophie: Both smiling!
Me: OMG! Send a picture.

When Sophie texted the picture of them to me, I asked Ms. Baumann if I could finish "helping" at dance practice early so I could go over there, and she said yes. Then Sophie asked her mom if she'd come pick me up. It was kind of cool. I felt like a movie star waiting for my car service to arrive, even though I was a girl in a leg cast incapable of walking the few blocks. When I hobbled into Gaga's bedroom, she smiled.

"Gaga, I was so worried about you." I leaned my crutches against the wall and sat down on the bed next to her.

Gaga took my hand in hers. Her fingers felt too thin and bony. "I'm glad you're here." Her voice sounded weaker than I would have liked.

"You scared us all," I told Gaga. "I'm not ready for you to die." I said the words softly so the nurse who was sitting in the chair on the other side of the room couldn't hear me. "My most important teen years are coming up, and

I'm counting on you to be around to give me good advice." I waited, unsure if or how Gaga would respond.

She actually laughed. It was a teeny, tiny laugh, more like a hiccup, but it was a laugh. "I hope I'll be around for a while too." Gaga paused and then gently squeezed my hand. "But if I'm not, you have all the smarts you need to make great decisions for yourself."

"Don't talk like that," I said to Gaga. It made me emotional to think about the possibility of her not being around.

I think Gaga could tell because she extended her pinkie toward mine. "Pinkie swear you'll remember what I said."

I was so surprised, I laughed. "Gaga, I didn't know you knew how to pinkie swear."

Gaga gave me a small smile. "I've watched you girls do it for years," she said. "It's my first time. But it's never too late to try something new."

Even though Gaga was weak, as we shook our pinkies together, I felt every ounce of her strength.

8:03 p.m.
Called Leo

I called Leo tonight to tell him about Gaga's recovery. "Science isn't always accurate," I said. "What you told me about the body breaking down was incorrect."

Leo said he's never been so glad to be proven wrong.

Wednesday, April 29, 6:42 p.m.
Sophie came over

I had a surprise visit tonight from Sophie. When she showed up on my front porch, I thought for sure she'd come to deliver bad news about Gaga in person. But she assured me Gaga actually had a good day. "She ate scrambled eggs," she said like that was Exhibit A of how well she was doing. "Can I come in?" Sophie asked. It was pretty clear she hadn't come to talk about Gaga's food intake.

"I had an amazing afternoon with Billy," she said as we sat down on my bed. "We went on a run and then to get smoothies."

"I didn't know either of you ran."

Sophie grinned. "We spent more time drinking our smoothies. Then we had a long talk."

I raised a brow, waiting to hear the details.

"We talked about a lot of stuff. Him. Me. How we feel about each other. He told me he's really going to miss me when I move back to New York. I told him I'm going to miss him too. He said it sucks that we have to break up just because I'm moving."

As Sophie talked, she blushed. I knew there had to be more. "Did something else happen?" I asked.

"I came to a realization," said Sophie. "Billy doesn't want to break up and neither do I." Words were coming out of her mouth at a much faster pace than usual. "I don't see why Billy and I have to break up when I leave. We can still go out even though he'll be in Faraway and I'll be in New York."

I didn't want to seem doubtful, but I had to ask the question in my brain. "How's that going to work?"

"Simple," said Sophie. "It's called a long-distance relationship."

Sophie sounded more grown-up than teenager, and it was odd. "Isn't that pretty complicated for a pair of fifteen-year-olds?" I shrugged like maybe I was just too juvenile to get it. "I mean, what would you do? Travel back and forth?"

Sophie frowned at me. "This wasn't supposed to be a conversation about logistics," she said. "I just wanted you to know how I'm thinking."

"Got it," I said.

Though to be honest, I didn't get it all.

Friday, May 1, 10:44 p.m.
Talked to Leo (54 minutes)

Leo called tonight. He said he was calling for a Gaga report. But after I told him that she seems to have stabilized, we talked for an additional fifty-three minutes, which makes me think he wasn't just calling because he wanted to check in on my ailing grandmother. Leo and I have been talking a lot lately, and our conversations have gotten longer and more flirtatious. Tonight, we talked about our favorite things.

"Favorite candy bar?" he asked.

"Definitely Reese's Peanut Butter Cups."

Leo made a buzzer sound like I'd given the wrong answer. "Technically not a bar."

I giggled. "Then Butterfingers."

"Yum," said Leo. "But Nestlé Crunch are better."

"I'd eat both," I said.

"Me too. Favorite band?"

That was an easy question. "Coldplay."

"Have you forgotten about the Beatles and the Rolling Stones?" Leo asked like it was difficult to understand how I could not have chosen either of those bands.

"Still Coldplay," I said.

Leo snorted like I was crazy, then he moved on to the next question. "Favorite month?"

"Any but April."

Leo laughed at my quick answer. He'd already heard my bad birthday curse theory and refuted it based on lack of any scientific proof that karma actually exists. "Aren't you going to ask my favorite month?" he asked.

"Sure," I said. "What's your favorite month?"

"May," said Leo without hesitation. "Can you guess why?"

"Because you'll be done with exams?" He'd been studying incessantly for finals.

"That's one reason," said Leo. "But there's another. Want a hint?"

"Sure," I said.

"Well," said Leo slowly. "This May when I come home from school, I'll get to spend a lot of time hanging out with a pretty, sweet girl."

I was surprised and a little embarrassed. He's not usually so openly flirtatious. "Does this girl have a name?" I asked.

"Actually, her name is April," he said.

I thought about how I've never liked the sound of my name. Until now.

I hope your rambles have been sweet,

and your reveries spacious.

—*Emily Dickinson*

Saturday, May 2, 8:45 p.m.
Home from Regionals
Exciting day

Even though I couldn't compete in the regional dance meet with my leg in a cast, it was still exciting to be with the team when we came in first place. We were all cheering and hugging when we found out we'd won and that we're advancing to the state meet. Even Ms. Baumann was in high spirits. And the excitement didn't end there. When I got home, May and June were literally waiting at the front door for me.

"April, I get to go to camp this summer!" June told me before I'd even had a chance to go inside. "There's a new program at Silver Shores for eight-year-olds, and Mom and Dad said I could do it!" She held her hand up and May high-fived it.

"That means we'll all be together," said May like she wanted to make sure I understood the full implication of what June was saying.

"I'm not going back to camp, May." We'd discussed this plenty of times. I shouldn't have had to remind her.

"But now you have to go back," she said, like the fact that June was going changed everything. "This is the last summer you can be a camper, which means it's the only chance we'll ever have to all be together at camp." May crossed her arms and looked at me. It was clear she wasn't giving up so easily.

"I've already decided," I told May. "I don't even know why we're discussing this."

May gave June a do-your-thing look. June

reached over and wrapped her arms around me. "Please, April! Please go back. We'll all have so much fun together."

My sisters weren't making this easy. I took in a deep breath and exhaled before I spoke. "It would be fun, but you and May will have plenty of fun without me," I said. What I didn't say was that her idea of fun and mine weren't exactly the same.

"We can talk about it later," said June.

I felt kind of bad. It was pretty obvious she didn't want to take *no* for an answer.

10:17 p.m.
Talked to Leo (43 minutes)

Tonight Leo called during his "phone break."

"Is that like a coffee break?" I asked.

Leo laughed. "I don't know. I don't drink coffee, so I've never taken a coffee break."

Even though he was studying for exams, I could tell he was in a playful mood.

"What exactly is a phone break?" I asked.

Leo explained that he made a study schedule for himself to get through exam week and that he had actually included time for phone breaks.

"I'm flattered," I said when he told me all his phone breaks were allotted to me. "What about your parents? Aren't you going to talk to them?"

"Nope," said Leo. "No phone breaks for them." I could hear the smile in his voice. "They know I'm busy studying."

"Leo, would you rather talk to me than your parents?" I feigned surprise.

Leo laughed. "Easy question. Absolutely."

I could tell he didn't mind my line of inquiry, so I continued. "How long did you allot for our phone breaks?"

"Now that's a good question," said Leo. "After careful review of the amount of studying I need to do, I allotted twenty minutes per break."

I looked at my phone. We'd been on for seventeen minutes. "Then we'd better start saying our good-byes. You've only got three minutes left."

Leo laughed.

"What's so funny?"

"I miscalculated," said Leo.

"You?" We both knew he almost never made mistakes when it came to anything scientific or mathematical. "What did you miscalculate?" I asked.

"The amount of time I'd want to talk to you."

We spent the next twenty-six minutes talking about how great it's going to be when we're both done with school and he's home for the summer. "I can't wait to hang out with you," said Leo. He'd said that before, but this time he sounded like he really meant it.

"Yeah, me too," I said softly.

Sure, I'll miss some things about camp. But all I want to do this summer is hang out with Leo.

10:52 p.m.
In bed

What was I thinking? I can't actually spend every day this summer just hanging out with Leo.

Leo will be working days at the deli, and I need something to do too. No way would Mom and Dad let me just sit around all day, and I wouldn't want to. But the question is: What am I going to do in Faraway, Alabama, all summer?

As I see it, I have three options.

I could ask Mom if I could work at her store. It's next door to the deli where Leo works. Even though a summer of folding clothes doesn't sound like the most exciting way to pass the time, it would be cool to work next door to Leo. We could take our breaks together.

I could ask Dad if I could work at the diner. Waiting tables wouldn't be so bad. I know he'd make me do lots of menial tasks like washing dishes. But I could ask Dad if I could spend some time in the kitchen too. It would be fun to gain some pie-making skills.

Or I could get a job somewhere else.

I can't help what I'm about to write, but wondering what I will be doing here this summer makes me think about what I would be doing if I went back to camp.

After what happened last summer, I told myself I wasn't going back. But the truth is that canoeing and swimming sounds like more fun than folding clothes or wiping down tables or whatever else I might end up doing.

Plus, I can't help but think about my sisters and the fact that this is the only summer that all three of us would be able to be there together.

I don't know why I'm thinking like this.

I had a terrible summer last year at camp and have no interest in repeating it, plus I want to be in Faraway with Leo. There's nothing else to think about.

Good night.

Tuesday, May 5, 7:43 a.m.
Happy birthday, May!

May's birthday is today, and she woke up everyone in our house this morning by shouting, "I'm twelve!" I got out of bed and went to her room.

"It's way too early for this much enthusiasm," I said. Even though she'd woken me from a deep sleep, when I saw her smiling face, I couldn't be mad at her.

"April, I'm twelve!" she shouted as she jumped up and down on her bed like a little kid.

"Happy birthday!" I said. The truth is that even if I hadn't had my leg in a cast, I wouldn't have gotten on the bed and jumped with her. From my own experience, I knew the probability was high that the year ahead of her will suck. I thought it was incredibly mature of me not to tell her.

"We're having my favorite dinner tonight— steak and baked potatoes. Mom is making a cake. And my party is Saturday at Sportz Town!" screamed May.

"That's a lot to be excited about," I told May as I left her room to go to my own and get dressed. Oddly, her early-morning enthusiasm was infectious. Now I feel excited too. It's May's birthday. Mom said Gaga seems to be doing OK. Leo is home on Thursday. I get my cast off on Friday, and

May's party is on Saturday. That's a lot to be happy about.

I don't always say this, but the week is shaping up to be a good one.

Do not pity the dead, Harry.

Pity the living.

—*Albus Dumbledore*

Thursday, May 7, 5:32 p.m.
Home

I should have known there was a real problem when Mrs. Monteleone called me to her desk in the middle of ninth-period history. "Sweetheart, you're going to need to go to the office."

It was weird. As far as teachers go, Mrs. Monteleone is one of the nicer ones, but still, I'd never heard her call anyone *sweetheart.* "Did I do something wrong?" I asked.

"I'm sure you didn't," she said.

"What was that about?" Emily, who sits next to me in history class, whispered as I collected my books.

I shrugged and pointed to my cast. "I'm supposed to go to the doctor tomorrow to get it off. Maybe my mom changed the appointment to today and forgot to tell me."

"That's probably it," said Emily.

But it was weird to be called out of class, and one look at Dad's face when I got to the office told me this had nothing to do with a broken bone. "What's the matter?" I asked.

Dad took my backpack from me and we walked down the hall together. When Dad didn't answer my question, I thought about probing him, but I didn't want to. I knew what he was going to say and I wanted to postpone hearing it as long as possible.

When we got to his car, Dad helped me into the passenger seat. I watched in the rearview mirror as he walked behind the car. "April, Gaga died this afternoon," he said when he was settled into the driver's seat. He reached over and squeezed my hand.

When I didn't move, he leaned over and hugged me.

I don't remember if I hugged him back. I don't remember what happened next. I don't know what I did or thought or said. The only thing I know for sure is that I cried as Dad drove to the middle school to get May and then to Faraway Elementary to get June.

I remember him repeating to May and June what he'd said to me, and I remember crying fresh tears every time I heard those words.

My sisters cried too. At some point between the elementary school and home, I asked Dad the question that had been forming in my mind for the whole ride. "How could this happen? Gaga was doing better. I don't get how she just suddenly died."

Dad looked pained as he answered my question. I know he was sad, and it must have made him even sadder to see May, June, and me so upset. "Sometimes people bounce back right before they die, like a final hurrah," he said.

"Why?" asked June.

Dad was quiet for a long time, contemplating

his answer. "I can't explain it," he finally said. "Maybe a person knows they're about to go, and they do whatever they can to have a little more time with the people they love."

When Dad said that, May, June, and I all started crying again.

"I'm sorry," Dad said. "I didn't mean to upset you with my answer."

"When is the funeral?" asked May. I hadn't even thought about that. And as it turned out, it was ironic that she was the one who asked the question, because the answer affected her in a very personal way.

"Her funeral is Saturday afternoon." Dad looked into the rearview mirror at May. He didn't have to say what we were all thinking, which was that it was the day May's birthday party was scheduled for.

May looked down. "I don't care about my party. We could change the date . . . or just cancel it."

"I'm sorry," Dad said to May as we got out of the car at home.

I didn't want to hear what she said in

response. I came straight to my room, closed the door, and got into my bed, where I've been ever since. I didn't go to dance practice or even tell Ms. Baumann I wouldn't be there. When she hears the reason I didn't show, I'm sure she'll understand. When Mom got home, she came into my room, and the two of us lay on my bed together and cried. She stayed until we both stopped.

My eyes are dry, for now. But there's so much I don't understand. How did this happen? I know what Dad said about the last hurrah, but I'm not sure I believe it. When I woke up this morning, I felt happy. Gaga was doing better. Leo was coming home. It was going to be a good day.

Now, I don't know what to do with myself. Do I call Leo? Text Billy?

I'm fifteen, and Gaga is the first person I know who has died. It would be helpful if there was some kind of instruction manual: *What to Do When Your Grandmother Dies.*

Sadly, I'm about to become an authority on the topic.

When I came out of my room, all I wanted to do was eat dinner with my family, but Aunt Lilly, Aunt Lila, and Mom were in the kitchen making funeral arrangements.

It seemed like Gaga had barely died and they were already trying to figure out what to do with her body. As I filled a bowl with chicken and rice, it was literally making me nauseated to hear Aunt Lilly telling Mom and Aunt Lila about her conversation with the funeral-home director.

"Do we really have to be talking about this right now?" I pointed to my bowl. "I'm trying to eat."

Aunt Lilly replied, "April, this is a grown-up conversation. Maybe it's best if you take your dinner and leave the kitchen."

When she said that, something in me snapped. "You can't tell everybody what to do," I said.

"April!" Mom said my name like she wanted to make sure I didn't say more. But I had a lot more to say to Aunt Lilly. "Amanda, Harry, Sophie, and I all heard you say that *you* were the sister in charge of Gaga's end-of-life care." I emphasized the word *you* to make it clear how Aunt Lilly viewed her role.

I saw Mom and Aunt Lila exchange a look.

"April, everyone is emotional right now. Please calm down," said Mom.

But I wasn't capable of being calm. I pointed at Aunt Lilly. "When Gaga came home from the hospital, you tried to take over at her house, and it upset Willy. I know because Sophie told me." I paused. "You think you're in charge of everybody, but you're not." When I finished, I looked at Aunt Lilly. She opened her mouth like she was going to say something, but Mom held up a hand to stop her.

As I stood there, my eyes filled with fresh tears. I couldn't believe what I'd said. I knew it was disrespectful. But it was true.

Mom walked over to where I was standing and put an arm around me. "You need to apologize to Aunt Lilly," she said.

"I'm sorry," I mumbled, then Mom steered

me out of the kitchen. She seated me on the couch in the family room with my sisters and my bowl of chicken and rice.

When she went back into the kitchen, she closed the door, but I could hear the argument my mom and her sisters were having. Aunt Lila told Aunt Lilly she had no right to take charge of everything. Mom said they were all going to make decisions together. Aunt Lilly said she shouldn't get blamed for being helpful.

They went round and round. I felt horrible as I sat and listened to what they were saying to each other. It was bad enough that Gaga was gone, and more awful that Mom and her sisters were fighting.

And worst of all, it was my fault.

9:55 p.m.

Billy called me. His mom told him about Gaga and he wanted me to know that he was sorry. I know he was trying to be nice, but I didn't have much to say.

Then Sophie called. She said she and Emma were with Willy, who had been crying all night. "It makes me sad to see him so sad," said Sophie. Then she started crying too. I stayed on the phone with Sophie for a long time. When we finally hung up, I knew there was somebody I needed to call.

But when I did, I started crying. I didn't even say why I called, but Leo knew. "April, I'm so sorry," he said. "It's hard when someone dies."

He was right. It was. "I don't think I'm going to be able to hang out much this weekend." My voice was barely a whisper.

"It's OK," said Leo.

"Aren't you going to try to say some of the things you're supposed to say when someone loses a person they love?" I asked.

"There's nothing to say," said Leo.

Then he just sat there and listened while I told him about the day and cried into the phone.

Saturday, May 9, 9:45 p.m.
Gaga's funeral

I'm not sure where to begin to describe Gaga's funeral. The whole day was surreal, and

I don't feel capable of writing about it in full.
But a few things stood out.

The most important thing happened before
the funeral. Mom and her sisters made up,
and while not much could have made me feel
better today, that did.

My whole family was waiting in this little
room for the service to begin when Aunt Lilly
apologized to Mom and Aunt Lila for being
too take-charge.

"It's OK," said Aunt Lila.

"You're just being the good oldest sister that
you've always been," Mom added.

Then all three of them group-hugged and
cried. Watching them made me think that
the older and bigger you are, the more tears
you have.

There were other things that stood out too.

First, I wore the green sweater Gaga knitted
and gave to me on my fourteenth birthday. It
made me feel her presence around me. I was
going to wear Gaga's ski cap she gave me after
our ski trip, but May decided to trim her bangs
before the funeral and accidentally cut them

entirely off. She was upset, so I let her wear the cap. I was glad it made May feel better.

Second, it was amazing to see all the people who came to the funeral and to Aunt Lilly's house afterward. Most were people I knew, like Uncle Marty and Sam, Gaga's friends from the Happiness Movement, Billy and his family, Leo and his parents, everyone who works at the diner, and a bunch of our neighbors. But what stood out more were all the faces of the people I'd never even seen, and I think what really meant the most was hearing what they had to say about Gaga.

The manager of Winn-Dixie, where Gaga shopped, told Mom that Gaga always said even if there was another grocery in Faraway, she wouldn't shop at it. He said she was one of his nicest customers. And the lady who did Gaga's hair told Mom, Aunt Lilly, and Aunt Lila that every year, Gaga knitted something for her for Christmas and that she was one of the kindest people she'd ever known. A bunch of people said stuff about how special Gaga was. I can't even remember who said what. I just know that every time I heard someone say something nice about Gaga, it made me feel a tiny bit better.

The third thing I remember was that Brynn didn't come to the funeral. Her parents were there, and even though Brynn and I had hardly spoken since our fallout in January, part of me hoped she'd be there. I kept waiting, thinking she'd show up. She loved Gaga, and Gaga loved her. When we were little, we spent hours at Gaga's house piecing together her old sewing scraps. I think in my mind, Brynn was going to show up and say she was sorry about everything that happened this year between us. It seems like it would have been the perfect opportunity to make up. But that didn't happen. I know if Gaga was here, she'd tell me to reframe it. She'd say to find the positive. In this case, I don't know what that would be, and it makes me particularly sad that I can't talk to Gaga about it.

Fourth, Gaga's friends from the Happiness Movement gave an incredible speech. Most of them had been friends for over fifty years, and they said Gaga was one of the most positive people they've ever known and that she'd want everyone to smile for the life she led and not be sad she was gone. They all wore their Happiness Movement T-shirts, which, in a weird way, made me remember the day Gaga gave them out to everyone in our family and made us all members of the Happiness Movement. I was a little relieved knowing that when I got home, the bright yellow T-shirt would be tucked safely away in the bottom of my dresser drawer.

The fifth thing I remember was feeling particularly sad after the funeral when Sophie and I hugged. Usually I feel happy around Sophie, but when we hugged I thought about the thing that brought us together, Gaga and Willy's marriage. Now it's gone, and that left me with an overwhelming sad feeling that so many things in my life would just never be the same.

Last but not least, I got my cast off yesterday, which meant I didn't have to show up on crutches at Gaga's funeral. I'm still in a boot, which I have to wear for another two weeks. That said, it was a very small victory amid a huge loss.

Sunday, May 10, 9:02 a.m.
Still sad

When we got home from Aunt Lilly's house last night, I got right in bed. I was too exhausted to even wash my face or brush my teeth. But I couldn't sleep. My brain kept going over everything that happened yesterday. Then it started thinking about Gaga and how much I'm going to miss her. I cried so much at the funeral that I didn't think I had any tears left, but apparently I did. Lots of them. I literally cried myself to sleep, which I didn't even know was a real thing.

I hoped that when I woke up this morning, I'd feel less sad. It seemed like that was a reasonable thing to hope for after being so sad yesterday. But I don't. I never imagined a time when Gaga wouldn't be part of my life, and I still can't. I hate the idea that she's gone, that

I'll never be able to talk to her or laugh with her again.

When I got out of bed, I went to the kitchen. Mom had made pancakes like she does every Sunday morning. For as long as I can remember, it's been a Sinclair family tradition to see who can eat the most pancakes. I can't remember the last time I actually wanted to win that contest, so for years, I let May and June have the honor. They liked winning, which means they always wanted to play.

But this morning, no one was in the mood. We all sat there just picking at our pancakes. Finally, June broke the silence. "Mom, did Gaga make pancakes for you and your sisters when you were growing up?"

It was clearly the wrong question to ask. Mom put her head in her hand and started crying. We all got up to hug her.

"I'm sorry," said June. She looked like she was about to start crying too.

"It's OK," Mom finally said. "It's just going to take a while."

Then we all sat back down and ate pancakes, drank juice, and read the newspaper like everything was normal.

But it was pretty easy to see that nothing was normal at all.

No act of kindness, no matter how

small, is ever wasted.

—*Aesop*

Friday, May 15, 9:52 p.m.

~~Gaga's 81st birthday~~

What would have been Gaga's 81st birthday

Everywhere I look, I'm surrounded by things that remind me of Gaga.

Since her funeral, our kitchen counter is covered with pies and cakes, our refrigerator is filled with casseroles, and every tabletop is covered with plants or flowers people have brought by to pay their respects.

I keep thinking about what Gaga would say about everything.

April, I try my best to eat healthy, but who can resist a chocolate pie? April, why would anyone put carrots in their cake? They belong in a salad. April, what's the point of giving flowers? They barely last a week. Now a plant . . . that's a different story.

Our house has become a gathering place. Mom, Aunt Lilly, and Aunt Lila have been together here all week—drinking tea, sorting through Gaga's "affairs," as they're calling it, and greeting people who come by. Mom told me it's a healing process, but all the constant reminders have made me feel stuck in my sadness.

I've tried to distract myself and force my brain to focus on other things. I cleaned out my closet, organized my backpack, and even tried to develop a late-in-the-year interest in algebra. But nothing worked. I've just felt so sad since Gaga died and no matter what I do, I can't think about anything other than Gaga.

Last night, I talked to Dad about it.

"Time heals all wounds," he said.

"It's not healing mine," I told him.

Dad gave me a hug and told me it was going to require more time.

When I went to bed, I made a conscious decision to try and be less sad. I did it because today would have been Gaga's eighty-first birthday, and I know if she were here, she'd tell me life is too short to be sad.

Still, when I woke up this morning, I couldn't help wishing she were here so we could celebrate her birthday, and it made me feel even sadder.

And I wasn't the only one who was thinking about her birthday. When I went to the kitchen for breakfast, Mom was standing at the counter, buttering toast and blinking back tears. It was obvious she was thinking about Gaga too. It made me feel kind of helpless to see her standing there like that. I wasn't sure what to do.

"Are you OK?" I asked.

Mom got a jar of jam out of the refrigerator and starting smearing it on the toast. "You know, it would have been her eighty-first birthday today."

"I know."

Mom put down the knife she was using

and put her head in her hands. Usually it's the parent's job to make a child feel better, but Mom looked like she needed to be comforted. I went to her and gave her a big hug. "I'm sorry you're sad," I whispered.

"She loved you so much," Mom whispered in my ear.

I had to blink back my own tears. I didn't want to go to school with puffy eyes, but as I left the house, my heart felt heavy. All through my morning classes, I literally felt like my heart was a ten-pound weight inside my chest.

When I sat down for lunch with Harry and Sophie, it was pretty obvious they were having a hard time too. Harry motioned to our trays. Sophie's and his contained chicken fingers, and there was a tuna wrap on mine. "Do you think Gaga would have picked the chicken fingers or a wrap?" he asked.

"That's a random question," I said.

Harry frowned at me like he was disappointed in my answer. "Everyone has their process." He paused. "I think she would have picked chicken fingers."

"I agree," said Sophie.

They both looked at me like I should weigh in. "She loved fried chicken," I said, even though I was pretty sure Faraway High's version wouldn't have appealed to her.

Sophie pursed her lips. "Did she like wraps?"

Harry and Sophie both looked at me again, like I would know best. But I had no idea. I'd never seen Gaga eat one. Still, it didn't mean she wouldn't have. I thought about what Mom had said before I left the house. I felt awful that Gaga loved me so much and I couldn't even answer a simple question about her, like if she liked wraps or not.

"I don't know," I said honestly. Then I picked up my wrap and took a bite. I didn't want to keep talking about Gaga.

Apparently, neither did Harry or Sophie. We all ate in silence. They finished their chicken fingers, but all I could do was pick at my wrap. I ended up dumping most of it in the trash. Even though I barely ate, I had a stomachache all afternoon. I tried to pay attention in my classes, but everything my teachers said swirled around me like they were speaking in Chinese or Russian or some other language I couldn't understand.

The dance team meeting after school wasn't much better. Ms. Baumann wanted to go over last-minute details for schedules, transportation, and costumes for the state meet tomorrow, and I was having a hard time paying attention to what she was saying.

Maybe it's because I still can't dance, which means I'm going along just to give moral support. But honestly, as she went on and on about making sure no one's bra straps were sticking out of their costumes, I wanted to scream, *"You're worried about bra straps when I'm sitting here thinking about my dead grandmother's birthday!"*

When the meeting ended, all I wanted to do was go home. Then, as I was leaving, I got a text from Leo.

Leo: Want to hang out?
Me: Sure.
Leo: Cold Shack?

Me: See you in ten.
Leo: I'll be there.
Me: :-)

I don't know why I said yes when only moments earlier I'd been so anxious to go home.

"What's going on?" he asked as soon as he saw me.

I knew I couldn't hide how I was feeling from him. When we sat down in a booth with our ice cream, I told him that today would have been Gaga's birthday and that I couldn't stop thinking about her. "She's been on my mind ever since she died. But especially today." I paused. "I want to find a way to just forget about it so I'll stop feeling sad."

Leo was quiet as he took a bite of his chocolate peanut butter ice cream. "Perhaps forgetting about it is the opposite of what you need to do."

I raised a brow at him. "What do you mean?"

"I think you need to remember everything you can about Gaga. Especially today. I say we celebrate her birthday."

I was confused. "Why would I want to do that?"

Leo shrugged. "You don't have anything to lose. It might make you feel better."

Leo had a point. But there was still something I didn't quite get. "How do we celebrate her birthday?" I asked quietly.

Leo took another bite of his ice cream. "Tell me about Gaga," he finally said.

It was a big question. I wasn't sure where to start. "What do you want to know?"

"Anything you want to tell me," said Leo.

I took a bite of my coffee fudge chip ice cream as I formulated my thoughts. I wasn't sure I'd want to say much, but once I started talking, I couldn't stop.

I told Leo how when I was little, Gaga used to save her stale bread and take me to Oakland Park to feed it to the ducks. I told him that May, June, and I stayed at her house for a week when Mom and Dad went out of town, and that she let us stay up late every night watching TV in her bed. I told him how she always did and said things that were so unexpected—

especially as she got older. "She took up running and got married at eighty. She started the Happiness Movement with her friends." I paused. "She even learned to snow ski after she was diagnosed with cancer."

Leo didn't interrupt as I spoke.

I told him how she had so much wisdom about life and always shared it with her family when they needed it. I told him that when Matt broke up with me, she cheered me up by teaching me how to knit and telling me all of her funny, crazy theories about boys. And then when I broke my leg skiing, she made me feel better by sharing her personal life story with me and explaining how she thought what she learned might be helpful to me. "Gaga always made me feel understood and loved," I told Leo.

When I finished talking, Leo smiled. "I feel like I got to know Gaga through you. Lucky me," he said. "She sounds like an incredible and unique person."

I exhaled. I don't know if it was from telling him everything I did or from hearing what he said, but either way, for the first time since the funeral, I felt lighter and happier. "Thanks," I said.

"For what?" asked Leo.

It made me smile. He's so smart. He knew exactly what he'd done, but I think he wanted me to say it. "For making me remember instead of trying to forget."

Leo nodded like it was the right answer. "We should get a cupcake in honor of Gaga's birthday."

"We've already had ice cream," I reminded him.

Leo grinned. "Last time I checked it was tradition to have cake and ice cream on your birthday."

"Good point," I said. So Leo and I went up to the counter and bought a cupcake, then we sat on a bench outside the Cold Shack and ate it.

"Would Gaga have liked me?" Leo asked as we licked sticky icing from our fingers.

"Totally." I bit my lip. "Just like I do." I wondered if it was wrong to be so openly flirtatious on Gaga's birthday, but I'm pretty sure she would have approved. And it seemed fitting that Leo found a way to cheer me up when I was down. He has a unique gift for doing that.

Just like Gaga.

Life is not measured by the number of breaths we take, but by the moments that take our breath away.

—Unknown

Saturday, May 16, 5:02 p.m.
Home from state competition
Feeling mixed

When I was with Leo yesterday celebrating Gaga's birthday, I felt happier than I had in a long time. As I went to bed, I felt certain the dark cloud that had been hanging over me had lifted, but I was wrong.

This morning, I left on a 5:30 a.m. bus with the dance team to go to the state competition in Birmingham. Even though we left at an hour when no one should be awake, everyone was super pumped on the ride there.

The team high continued all day while we waited for our turn to perform, and then while the other teams performed, and especially when the results were announced and we learned the Faraway team came in first place.

Everyone on my team was cheering and going wild.

I acted like I was excited too—but it was just acting. I wanted to seem happy we'd won, and I was. But when we heard we'd won, my first thought was that I wouldn't be able to share the good news with Gaga. I felt like I had a secret I couldn't share with my teammates.

What would I have said?

6:10 p.m.
Talked to Billy

OMG! Billy just called and I can't believe what he told me.

"Sophie and I hung out this afternoon, and she invited me to spend the summer with her in New York City."

"WHAT?" Sophie hadn't mentioned a thing about this to me, and I honestly wasn't even sure what it meant.

"You heard me," said Billy.

"Huh? She wants you to come to New York for the summer?" I asked.

"Yeah. Sophie told me she'd been thinking about it and that she'd come up with a way for us to spend the summer together." Billy paused. "She's going to an arts day camp and said I could find something to do in the city too—like go to a camp, get a job, or volunteer somewhere. She told me I could even go to a student-government camp and learn how to better represent my school. She said there are tons of things to pick from, and that I could stay at her mom's or her dad's apartment."

I was shocked to hear she'd suggested all this. I could tell Billy was too. He kept talking. "She said this way, we wouldn't have to break up, and that it would be the first step in having a long-distance relationship."

I took a deep breath. Sophie is normally so

reasonable, but this sounded crazy. "What did you tell her?" I asked Billy.

"First, I told her I was already planning to go back to Camp Silver Shores."

That made sense. It was the truth. "Did she understand?"

"Not really," said Billy. "She said that given the circumstances of her having to move back to New York City because her parents are getting divorced and both wanting custody of her, she hoped I'd be understanding and think about changing my plans."

That sounded like something Sophie might say. Especially lately. "What did you say to that?" I asked.

"I told her my parents would never let me do that."

That was also the truth. "That was a good thing to say," I told Billy.

"It didn't help," he said. "She told me I didn't have to give her an answer today. She said take some time to think about it, and that I should try to think outside the box."

"Not 'think outside the bun'?" I couldn't

help being a little sarcastic. Billy laughed. He knew the Taco Bell commercial too.

"Is there any part of you that wants to do it?" I asked Billy. He's really into Sophie, so I thought it was a question worth considering.

But apparently Billy didn't need any time to formulate his answer. "No," he said. "I don't want to go to New York for the summer. I want to go to camp. But I also don't want to hurt Sophie's feelings. She's going through a lot."

I've known Billy a long time. The thing he hates most is confrontation, which is why I knew the only thing he'd done today was avoid one.

11:17 p.m.
#bestnightever

At the risk of sounding overly dramatic, I want to say that as sad as I was at the state meet all day is as ecstatic as I am right now. I'm literally bursting with happiness. I know that sounds like someone else found my journal and is writing in it, but it's true.

What happened tonight was AMAZING!

I went to see a movie with Leo, and as we walked back to my house together, he was very quiet. At first, I wondered if there was a problem. "Is something wrong?"

"There's something I want to talk to you about," said Leo.

"What?" I asked.

When he said he wanted to be sitting down when we talked, my mind started to race. As we looked for a bench, I did a mental review of our night to try and figure out what I might have said or done wrong.

Then I started thinking that the problem might be bigger than something that happened tonight. I was scared he was going to say that ever since he came home, I've been in a dark place, and that it's been kind of a bummer. I didn't really think he'd say that, but it was true, so I kind of got why he might.

As we sat, Leo looked pale and I noticed beads of sweat on his forehead. He was clearly nervous. "If you have something to say, just say it," I said.

"Actually, there's something I want to do," said Leo. Then he leaned over and kissed me. I'd kissed him before, when he told me he didn't know how, but this kiss felt different. When Leo pulled back, he looked at me. He still looked kind of nervous, but not as much as he had before we kissed. "I have something for you," he said, then he reached into his back pocket and showed me a piece of paper.

When I read it, I couldn't believe what I was seeing. It was the definition of the word *girlfriend*, complete with synonyms!

girl·friend: 1 / ˈgərlˌfrend/ noun
a female companion with whom a person has a romantic relationship.
Synonyms: sweetheart, partner, significant other, girl, woman, steady, (main) squeeze, boo, GF, lady friend, ladylove

"April, I've never had a girlfriend," said Leo. He looked at me and took my hand in his. "Will you be my first?"

"Yes," I said happily. "I'd love to be your girlfriend."

Then we kissed again. It was our first official kiss as boyfriend and girlfriend and it was perfect. Leo wrapped his arms around my waist as my hands settled on the back of his neck. We kissed like that for a long time, until he walked me home. When we got to my house, he kissed me good night. "Day one of being boyfriend and girlfriend has been great," Leo said.

I laughed and told him I thought so too.

Part of me worried that kissing Leo as his girlfriend would be awkward, but it wasn't.

When Billy asked me out, we'd been friends for so long, and even though the idea of having a boyfriend was exciting, it was weird to be more than friends with him.

Then when Matt asked me out, I was excited, but I knew my family wouldn't be. I never felt like I knew who he was or how he felt about me. And whenever we made out, I always had an unsettling feeling that he wanted to go further than I did.

But now, there's Leo. I'm excited we have
a whole, hot summer to hang out and have
fun. I might sound like Goldilocks when she
sat in Baby Bear's chair and ate his porridge
and slept in his bed . . . but going out with Leo
feels just right.

In every job that must be done, there

is an element of fun.

—*Mary Poppins*

Sunday, May 17, 9:17 a.m.
Pancakes and planning

When I woke up, I went straight to the kitchen. But I had a lot more than pancakes on my mind. I waited until everyone had finished and Mom was the only one left in the kitchen. She seemed kind of deep in thought, so I wasn't sure if it was a good time. But I had something important I needed to talk to her about.

"Want some help?" I asked as she washed dishes.

"Sure," she said. But when she handed me a wet serving bowl, it slipped through my fingers and fell to the floor, breaking off several big chips from the edge. Mom groaned as she bent down to pick up the pieces. "You should be more careful," she snapped.

It was easy to see she was upset.

"I'm sorry," I said. "It was an accident." I tried to help Mom clean up the mess, but she stopped me.

"I got it," she said like she really didn't want my help.

Even though I wanted to talk to Mom, it didn't seem like a very good time. "I can go," I offered.

Mom sighed. "I'm sorry. I have a lot on my mind this morning. Please stay and keep me company," she said as she finished cleaning up the broken pieces.

"Are you thinking about Gaga?" I asked.

Mom nodded. "I miss her."

"Me too." I took a dish towel from the drawer by the sink and started to dry what Mom had washed. I think it was therapeutic for her because when we finished, she looked at me and smiled. "I know my daughter. I can tell there's something on your mind."

I was relieved Mom was acting like Mom again. I really needed to talk to her. "I've been thinking about the summer," I told Mom. "I'm not going back to camp."

Mom frowned like she didn't like hearing me say that so definitively.

She, Dad, and I had had a long talk about the fact that this was the last summer I could go to camp. Their feeling was that I shouldn't *not* go just because I had a bad experience last summer, especially since both of my sisters are going. They had asked that I give it some serious thought, and now I had.

"I want to be in Faraway this summer," I said before Mom could argue with me. "And I was thinking it might be a good experience for me to work at your store."

Mom looked at me. I could tell I surprised her. I get why. She knows that normally I would think anything, even cleaning out the garage or eating raw broccoli, would be more fun than helping the ladies of Faraway assemble outfits. I knew I owed her a little bit of an explanation, especially since I was the one asking for a job.

"Leo and I are going out," I said. I could feel myself starting to blush as I told Mom about my new status. "He's working at the deli this summer, and I want a job in Faraway too."

Mom smiled. "April, that's so exciting. Leo is so nice."

"Thanks," I said, unsure what the right response was.

I guess Mom sensed my hesitation to continue talking about Leo and switched topics. "I could definitely use the help," she said. "If you work at the store, your hours would be ten to four Monday through Friday. You'd have to come neat, clean, and ready to work. You'd be folding clothes, assisting customers, and helping with inventory control. And you'd make minimum wage." Mom stopped talking and looked at me. "How does that sound?"

It took no time for me to think it through. "Great!"

Mom smiled. "I look forward to having you around this summer!"

"I look forward to being around," I told her. Even though I'll be working, it will be fun to make money during the day and hang out with Leo at night.

I can't believe I'm about to say this, but it doesn't even sound like work.

10:03 a.m.
Snooping sisters .

"We heard your conversation," said May as soon as I walked out of the kitchen after my talk with Mom.

"Yeah," June added. "You're NOT going to camp."

She said the word *not* like I was doing something wrong.

Instead of addressing what I wasn't doing, I decided to focus on what I would be doing. "I'll be working at Mom's store," I said.

"Leo is your boyfriend now?" said June. It was more question than statement, and I really didn't want to answer it.

"You two were eavesdropping!"

"No we weren't," said May. "We just overheard what you said."

June rolled her eyes at May. "That's what eavesdropping means," she said, like May must not know.

May ignored her. "Why don't you want to go back to camp?"

"Yeah," said June. "Why don't you want to go?"

As they stood there looking at me, I knew they wouldn't understand why I wanted to be in Faraway with my boyfriend. "I'm sorry I won't be there," I said in response to their question. "You'll still have a great time without me."

June frowned. "It would be more fun with you."

"Yeah," said May. "It really would be."

I didn't have a response for that.

10:32 a.m.
Thinking

When May and June asked if Leo was my boyfriend, it made me realize there are other people I should tell, and the person's name at the top of that list is Sophie.

I feel bad even writing this, but part of me doesn't want to tell her. When I do, she's going to ask what I'm doing this summer. How's that conversation supposed to go when a.) she hasn't even told me she invited Billy to New York for the summer, and b.) I know (but she doesn't) that he's not planning to go?

She's going to find out sooner vs. later. We have final exams this week, and then she and Emma leave on Sunday to go back to New York. Billy has to tell her he's not coming before she leaves. I know I need to tell her my news too.

The only question is: when?

11:19 p.m.
Talked to Leo

Leo just called, and I told him about my conversation with Mom.

"Awesome!" he said.

I'd never heard him use that word before,

and it sounded funny coming out of his mouth. "We'll both be downtown. We can meet for lunch or coffee."

"I highly approve of lunch," said Leo. "You know I don't drink coffee." I could hear the teasing in his voice.

"We can go to yoga after work," I added.

"Now you're talking," Leo said like he approved of that aspect of the plan.

He might be most excited about yoga, but the whole idea of a summer with my sweet, funny, chemistry-genius boyfriend sounds appealing.

Then I told Leo that I had to go because I had to study. There's only one thing that stands between a perfect summer and us—my final exams.

But that's a pretty big thing.

5:48 p.m.
Talked to Sophie

All day I've been studying bio, but my mind kept drifting from what's in my textbook to thoughts of Sophie. I had to tell her about Leo.

"How's the studying going?" I asked when

I finally called. We both have our bio exam on Tuesday, so it seemed like a good place to start the conversation.

"Pretty good," said Sophie. "Do you think we should study together tomorrow?"

"Sure," I said. I'd thought about asking her too. We're in the same class, and we'd been studying for bio tests together all year. I had just been avoiding asking because I didn't want to have to tell her about Leo.

But she's my best friend, and I'd be hurt if the roles were reversed and she didn't tell me she was going out with someone. I had to tell her.

"I have some news." My voice sounded too much like a TV news announcer. I took a deep breath to calm myself down. It was ridiculous that I was anxious to tell Sophie about Leo. I decided to just be direct and say it. "Leo asked me out."

"Wow!" said Sophie. "When?"

It was a fair question. Any friend would want details, but I knew exactly what was about to happen.

"Last night," I said. "After the movie."

There was a long pause on Sophie's end of the phone. "Why didn't you call and tell me last night?" she asked.

"I got home late. I was so tired." It sounded like a lie, even to me.

"How come you didn't call me earlier today?" she asked.

"I'm sorry. I started studying bio and I lost track of time." I didn't want to tell her the real reason I hadn't called.

I wasn't sure if Sophie believed me or not, but she let it go. "I'm happy for you," she said. We chatted for a few minutes about Leo, but as we made a plan to meet tomorrow to study, I think it was pretty obvious to both of us that there was only one way to describe the way our conversation felt.

Weird.

Monday, May 18, 5:32 p.m.
Studied with Sophie

Sophie and I spent the last four hours together studying bio. We talked about everything from ecology to ecosystems, but the one thing we didn't discuss was the reason for the obvious tension between us. I had to address it as we packed up our books. "I'm sorry I didn't tell you sooner about Leo."

"Yeah, that," said Sophie like it was now officially a topic. "I keep asking myself why you wouldn't tell me right away." She shrugged. "And I can't come up with a reason."

This was exactly what I'd been dreading. I had to be honest. "I guess I felt guilty."

"Why?" asked Sophie.

I suddenly realized I was in a predicament. Sophie still hadn't told me she'd asked Billy to spend the summer with her in New York. I couldn't let her know Billy had told me. "Because I'll be in Faraway with Leo this summer and I feel bad that you're leaving and you won't get to spend the summer with Billy."

At first, I was relieved because Sophie started laughing. But then I was horrified at what she said. "I probably should have told you this," she said, "but I asked Billy to come to New York for the summer, and I'm pretty sure he's going to. He just has to talk to his parents." She waved her hand in front of her like it was a formality.

I pretended to scratch at a mosquito bite. I truly didn't know what to say. Part of me felt like I should tell Sophie the truth— which was that Billy probably wasn't going to go. But I also knew I couldn't betray his confidence.

I decided to take a path in the middle. "He already signed up to go to camp," I reminded her. "Do you think he'll change his plans?"

Sophie frowned like she didn't like my question. "You're going to have a fun summer with your boyfriend. You should be happy for me that I'm going to have one too."

"OK," I said. She really hadn't left me room to say much else.

Sophie grinned. "So you don't have to feel bad. We're both going to have awesome summers." Then she leaned over and hugged me.

She said I didn't need to feel bad, but I couldn't have felt worse.

7:32 p.m.
Called Billy

I really didn't want to be part of the Sophie/Billy summer drama. It's none of my business. But after talking to Sophie, I felt like I had to say something to Billy, so I called him. "She thinks you're going to New York," I told him.

I waited for Billy to respond, but he didn't. "You have to tell her," I said.

Billy groaned. "I know. But I don't want to do it until after finals. She needs to focus on her tests and I don't want to upset her."

"Sure," I said like that made sense. But the more I think about it, I'm not so sure waiting is the best approach.

Wednesday, May 20, 10:41 p.m.
Studied with Leo (and actually learned something)

Leo came over tonight to help me study algebra. We sat at the kitchen table, doing problem after problem, until I hit one I just couldn't figure out. I slammed my notebook shut. "This is so frustrating." I pretended to pull out my hair.

Leo re-opened my notebook. "Keep working. You just haven't figured it out yet."

I shut my notebook again. "I don't care if I ever figure it out. I hate algebra."

Leo smiled. "Algebra is cool."

Leo and I were about to have our first fundamental difference of opinion. "Snow skiing is cool. Snorkeling is cool. Taylor Swift is cool. Algebra is not cool."

Leo rolled his eyes. "Algebra is much cooler than Taylor Swift."

"How can you say that?" I asked. As we started to debate the coolness of algebra, I was sure I was going to win, but Leo said something that surprised me.

"Algebra is cool because it's about finding the unknown."

"That makes it sound a little more intriguing," I admitted. I re-opened my notebook and kept working on the problem until I solved it.

"Nicely done," said Leo. I grinned as he high-fived me.

I can't believe I sat for a year in class and it wasn't until now, the day before the final exam, that I had any clue what I was doing. One of the things I like best about Leo is that he always gives me a new and unique way of looking at things.

Even algebra.

Friday, May 22, 5:00 p.m.
On the couch
Watching SpongeBob
Happy as a clam (Ha! Underwater humor)

I'm done! One year of high school down; three to go.

If I had to rate it, I'd give it a six. And I think that's being generous. A lot of bad stuff happened—my best friend since kindergarten ended our friendship, I broke my leg, and my grandmother died. I could keep going, but the good news is that I'm done with school until the fall!

I'm tired from studying and taking tests all week, but I'm happy to be sitting on this couch, chilling with my sisters, watching dumb

TV, and knowing that I've got a fun summer ahead of me.

But not everything is going to be great. Especially this weekend.

Tomorrow, I'm helping Sophie pack. I know it will be sad boxing up all of her things, but it's going to be hard for another reason too. She's going to be upset when she finds out Billy isn't coming to New York. I'm going to be there for her, but I'm not sure my presence is going to make her feel better. She's going to say that I'm spending the summer with Leo so I can't understand how she feels. I really hope that's not the case.

Then Sunday, we're having a going-away lunch at the diner for Emma and Sophie before they leave. It's going to be hard to say good-bye.

But today, I don't want to think about that.

My brain is ready for a break—I'd like to jump ahead to the part where the hardest thing I have to think about is helping the ladies of Faraway look their most fashionable.

Actually, that might be kind of hard too.

Nothing is so painful to the human mind as a great and sudden change.

—*Mary Shelley*, Frankenstein

Saturday, May 23, 4:42 p.m.
Helped Sophie pack

I helped Sophie pack today. As we folded piles of jeans, T-shirts, sweaters, and leggings, and boxed up all of her knickknacks, the reality of the fact that she's leaving tomorrow set in. Plus, I kept waiting for her to say something about Billy telling her he wasn't going to New York for the summer.

"Penny for your thoughts," said Sophie as she bubble-wrapped the plaque she'd gotten for being a student government rep.

"I have lots of them," I said. It was the truth.

Sophie put down the plaque and plopped onto her bed. She patted the space next to her. I sat and thought about what was on my mind.

She hadn't brought up Billy and I didn't want to be the one to do it. "I got so used to having you in Faraway. I can't imagine what it's going to be like when you're gone," I said.

Sophie rolled her eyes like I was being overly dramatic. "You have your dance-team friends."

I nodded. "But you're my bestie and I'm going to miss you like crazy."

Sophie linked her arm through mine. "I'm going to miss you too," she said. "You promised you're going to come visit me in New York."

"And leave Faraway?"

We both laughed at my joke. We'd talked about it before. I can't wait to get out of this little town and go visit her in New York City. I put my head on her shoulder and we sat like that for a long time, neither of us saying a word.

"What else are you thinking about?" she finally asked.

"It's sad being at Gaga's house," I said. It

was the first time I'd spent time there since she died, and it didn't feel right knowing she was gone and that Sophie was leaving soon too.

"I know," said Sophie. "It has been weird living here since she died."

I hadn't thought about how that must feel for Sophie. It can't have been easy. Hearing her say that made me glad I hadn't brought up the topic of Billy. She'd had a lot of sadness to deal with lately. Her parents getting divorced. Moving back to New York. Gaga dying and having to leave her grandpa alone in Faraway. I started thinking that relative to everything she's gone through lately, Billy telling her he's not coming to New York for the summer might not even be a big deal to her.

"April, there's something I need to tell you," said Sophie.

I mentally braced myself.

"Brynn apologized to me."

I stared blankly at Sophie, wondering if I'd misheard what she'd said. It wasn't at all what I'd expected.

I sat quietly as Sophie told me what

happened. "When Brynn heard I was moving back to New York, she told me she wanted to talk to me. She said she was sorry she'd been such a bad friend to me all year. She apologized for all the mean stuff she did."

"When did this happen?" I asked.

Sophie looked at me like she wasn't sure I was going to like what she was about to say. "After spring break. When we got back from the ski trip, I told Billy about the move. I guess word traveled fast, which is how Brynn heard." Sophie shrugged. "She told me she didn't want me to leave without saying she was sorry for how she acted."

I wasn't sure what shocked me more—the fact that Brynn apologized, or that Sophie hadn't told me for a whole month.

For that matter, it was equally shocking that Sophie hadn't brought up Billy. Then it hit me that maybe he hadn't told her. Though that seemed pretty unlikely since she's leaving tomorrow. I didn't know where to start.

"What did you say to Brynn?" I finally asked.

"I told her I appreciated it. What else could

I have said? That I wished she'd done it sooner so we could have been friends?" Sophie paused and looked at me. "I've been thinking about it for a while, and I thought you should know."

I wasn't sure what to do with that information. Brynn apologized to Sophie and not to me, so I didn't really see how it changed anything between the two of us.

"Is there anything else you want to tell me?" I asked, my brain switching from the topic of Brynn to Billy.

Sophie frowned. "Like what?"

"Nothing," I said. Sophie had concealed Brynn's apology from me for a long time. I thought we didn't have secrets between us, but clearly we do.

If she wasn't bringing up the topic of Billy, neither was I.

8:05 p.m.
Billy called

Now I know why Sophie didn't bring up the topic of Billy. She doesn't know he's not going to New York. The reason I know is because

Billy just called to ask me how I thought he should tell her.

"Billy! How could you not have told her yet?" I yelled.

"It's not exactly something she's going to want to hear," said Billy defensively.

"That's true," I said. "But it won't help to procrastinate. You just need to get it over with."

"This isn't homework," said Billy.

"I get it," I said. "She's going to be upset when she finds out."

"Right," said Billy like he was at least relieved that I understood his dilemma. "I was going to tell her Friday after finals. We went on a walk and got cupcakes. It was our last date together, I didn't want to spoil the day. Then, I was going to tell her today, but when I texted to see if I could come over, she said you were there helping her pack."

I reminded Billy of the timetable here. "She's leaving tomorrow. We have a family lunch at the diner, and then she and Emma are on a flight tomorrow night. You have to tell her before she goes."

"I know," said Billy. "I don't want to tell her tonight. It's a bad way to go to bed."

"If you'd already told her, this wouldn't be a problem." It was rare that I felt mad at Billy, but I was irritated he hadn't been more direct with Sophie.

"That doesn't help," said Billy. "I wish I'd told her, but I didn't. She was going through a lot. I didn't want to add to it."

"I'm sorry," I said. I hadn't meant to judge him. Telling people something they don't want to hear is hard. I thought about May's birthday, when Dad had to tell May and June and me that Gaga died. That must have been awful for him.

"I'm going to tell her in the morning," said Billy, interrupting my thoughts.

As I hung up the phone, I couldn't help but think that it's not going to make for a good start to her last day in Faraway.

Sunday, May 24, 6:09 p.m.
In my room

When I woke up this morning, if I'd known how terrible the day was going to

115

turn out, I would have just stayed in bed.

My family went to the diner for lunch. The point of the lunch was for everyone to have an opportunity to say good-bye to Sophie and Emma, not for Sophie and me to get in a fight, or for my whole family to witness it. But that's exactly what happened.

Sophie and Emma were the last to arrive at the diner. Dad had been there all morning, so May and June and I went over with Mom in time for lunch. Aunt Lilly and Uncle Dusty were already there with Harry and Amanda, and Aunt Lila and Uncle Drew had already arrived with Charlotte and Izzy. Dad had set up a table in a private room in the back. We were all starting to sit when Sophie, Emma, and Willy arrived. Sophie's eyes were puffy and her nose was red. It was easy to see she'd been crying.

"What's the matter?" I asked as she walked up to the table. Billy was going to talk to her this morning, so I was pretty sure that's what she was upset about.

But I was only half right.

"Why didn't you tell me Billy isn't coming to New York this summer?" she asked loudly enough that everyone in my family stopped talking and looked at her, then turned their attention to me like they wanted to hear my response.

I didn't like being in the spotlight, especially since I had no clue how to respond. The only way Sophie would know that I knew was if Billy told her he'd told me he wasn't going, and I couldn't imagine why he would do that.

"You're upset," I said.

"Yeah." But Sophie looked more mad than upset.

"Catfight," said Amanda.

"Amanda!" Aunt Lilly said her name like she had no place in the conversation.

"Why don't you tell me what happened?" I said.

Everyone looked at Sophie as she started to talk.

"You should know," she snapped. When I didn't respond, Sophie kept going. "Billy told me he's not coming to New York this summer.

When I asked him why he hadn't told me, he said he didn't want to upset me during finals."

Emma cleared her throat like she was purposely interrupting Sophie. "Why don't you and April take this outside."

Sophie ignored her mother's suggestion and continued to talk to me as if I was the only person in the room. "Billy should have told me sooner, but he didn't. I asked him if he'd talked to anyone else about it and he told me he didn't want to lie and that he'd talked to you. I get that he didn't want to upset me. But what I don't get is why you didn't tell me. You're supposed to be my best friend!"

"April, I agree with Emma," said Mom. "You girls need to discuss this privately."

"Stay," said Harry. "I'm enjoying it." He positioned himself in front of the door like he wanted to prevent us from leaving.

"Harry, not another word!" warned Aunt Lilly.

"Is April in trouble?" asked Charlotte.

"Is Sophie?" said Izzy.

No one answered their questions. Everyone

sat there, quietly looking at me like it was my turn to respond. "It wasn't my news to tell," I said to Sophie.

Her hands were on her hips as she faced me. "I get that. But it would have been nice if you'd given me a warning or something."

I crossed my arms across my chest and faced Sophie head on. It was unfair she was accusing me of something that wasn't true. "I tried," I said. I reminded her what I'd said the day we studied bio together. "I told you Billy was already signed up for camp and I asked if you thought he would really change his plans."

"We should eat," said Mom. "Sophie and Emma have a plane to catch." She handed a plate to Sophie and one to me and pointed us both to the buffet Dad had set up.

So we ate. It wasn't like we had a choice. But Sophie and I didn't say another word to each other the entire lunch. When it was over, Emma and Sophie said their good-byes before they left with Uncle Drew to go to the airport in Mobile.

Sophie and I hugged. But it was stiff and

awkward and not at all how I'd imagined our last day together would be.

When I got home, I made two phone calls. The first one was to yell at Billy. The second was to Leo to tell him what happened. "It was so weird. I've been dreading her leaving for such a long time because I thought it would be so sad. I never imagined we'd end up in our first big fight on her last day here."

I waited for Leo to respond. I thought he might say something honest, like, *"That's awful that you had a fight on her last day."* Or something reassuring. Or even something scientific yet entertaining, like telling me the average number of fights best friends get in. I knew whatever he said would make me feel better.

But all he said was, "Yeah, I get it."

Honestly, it didn't seem like he got it at all.

I don't understand it. The children are disappearing like rabbits.

—*Willy Wonka*

Monday, May 25, 4:15 p.m.
Jinxed

Now I know why Leo didn't have much to say when I called to tell him about Sophie. He had something he had to say to me.

Leo called a little while ago and said he wanted to come over and talk.

I thought for sure it would be about what happened with Sophie at the diner. He'd been strangely quiet when I told him about it. I figured he'd had time to think on things.

But that wasn't what he wanted to talk

about. When he showed up, we sat down on my front porch.

"April, there's something I need to tell you," said Leo.

"Do you have to have your tonsils removed?" I asked playfully.

"Nothing like that," said Leo. He flashed me a smile, but it was easy to see he was stressed.

"What is it?" I asked.

Leo inhaled and exhaled several times like I've seen him do in yoga class. "An opportunity has come up," he finally said.

"What kind of opportunity?"

"Remember I told you that my grandpa is a physicist and my grandma is a neurosurgeon?"

"Yeah." I knew they were both scientists, but I didn't know what kind or how it was relevant to our conversation.

Leo kept talking. "They're in town for a visit." He paused. He actually looked more nervous than he had when he asked me out. "Then they're spending the summer in Costa Rica where my grandma is doing research.

They invited me to join them for a month and do research in the lab with her."

Leo looked at me to see if I was following what he was saying. "It's an opportunity I can't refuse." I listened as he told me about how they would be studying brain activity and neural pathways in monkeys. Then, the impact of what he was saying hit me full force.

"You'd rather be researching monkey brains than spending the summer with me?"

"That's not a fair question," said Leo.

"You'll be gone most of the summer." It was a statement, but I was really asking it as a question, and Leo knew it.

He nodded.

My throat felt tight, like there was a wad of gum stuck in it. "We had a plan," I said, like it was wrong that he was changing it. "We were supposed to spend the summer together."

"I'm sorry," said Leo. "I know this isn't what you wanted to hear. Are you mad?"

"Yeah," I said, like it was pretty obvious why I would be.

I was mad at Leo for going away when we'd

decided to be together. I was mad at him for choosing monkey brains over me. But I was also upset that my summer I'd so carefully planned was pretty much ruined. Tears were starting to form in the corners of my eyes and I didn't want Leo to see me cry. "I have to go." Leo tried to grab my arm as I got up, but I jerked it away from him.

"April, wait! Can we talk about this?" he said.

I shook my head like there was nothing else to talk about.

Then I went inside, went to my room, and closed the door. I curled up on my bed with Gilligan and cried. I cried myself to sleep for the second time in less than a month.

When I woke up, Dad was sitting on my bed. "What's wrong with my number-one daughter?" he asked.

So I told him. Before he owned the diner, Dad wrote a relationship column. I knew he'd have something to say about how Leo was being a bad boyfriend for leaving me when we had plans to both be home this summer. But he didn't say anything like that.

"It doesn't seem quite fair, does it?" asked Dad.

It might not have been what I wanted to hear, but I couldn't argue with it. "No," I said as I put my head on Dad's shoulder. "It doesn't seem fair at all."

*The time has come for me to get my
kite flying, stretch out in the sun,
kick off my shoes, and speak my piece.*

—Harpo Marx

Wednesday, May 27, 1:59 p.m.
At the cemetery
At Gaga's grave

I came here today because I needed to talk
to Gaga. I mean, I knew she couldn't actually
talk back. But I told her what was on my mind,
and I tried to imagine what her responses
would be. Our conversation went something
like this:

*Me: Hi, Gaga. I came here today because I needed
to talk to you.*

Gaga: April, you can always talk to me.

Me: Even now?

Gaga: (laughing) Even now.

Me: A lot has happened since you've been gone. That makes it sound like you're somewhere exotic like Prague or Paris, or even somewhere nearby, like Birmingham, and that you're going to be back soon. I wish that were the case. There are other people I could talk to, but when I had really important things to talk about, you were my person.

Gaga: Smart choice!

Me: (waiting quietly for Gaga to stop laughing at her own joke)

Gaga: Sorry! So what brings you here today?

Me: A couple of things. First, Leo and I started going out.

Gaga: That's exciting!

Me: Yeah. It was. We had plans to spend the summer together, but then he told me he decided to go to Costa Rica to do research on monkey brains with his grandma.

Gaga: She sounds like an interesting grandma.

Me: I should have been happy for him. But when

he told me he was leaving, I got mad. That was immature, right?

Gaga: What do you think?

Me: I think if you were here, you'd say something like: "April, it's natural to be disappointed when things don't turn out the way you'd planned. I know you were looking forward to spending the summer with that boy, but you'll find a way to make the summer great." Or maybe: "This is a blessing in disguise. Him going away gives you the perfect opportunity to do something useful with your time, like improving your knitting skills."

Gaga: I wouldn't say that. I know you wouldn't want to spend your summer knitting.

Me: (laughing) There's more.

Gaga: I hope it's not serious.

Me: You know Brynn and I haven't spoken since January. She was mad Sophie and I became such good friends, and she got even madder when Billy and Sophie started going out. She hasn't spoken to either of them since January either. But the person she was most angry with was me.

Gaga: What a shame. I always liked Brynn.

Me: I don't know if I should tell you this, but she didn't even come to your funeral, which I thought was pretty wrong of her.

Gaga: People have their reasons.

Me: But she did apologize to Sophie for how she treated her. I know how much Brynn hates to apologize, so it must have taken a lot for her to do that.

Gaga: What are you going to do?

Me: I'm thinking about telling her I know about her apology to Sophie.

Gaga: You know what I always said. Trust your gut.

Me: I thought you were going to say everyone deserves a second chance.

Gaga: That too.

Me: I'll think about that, but there's one more thing I need to tell you. Sophie and Emma left three days ago, and Sophie and I had our first fight. It's unbelievable to me that Sophie lived here for a year and we were best friends. We almost always got along, and then the day that she left, we didn't. I don't want to sound dramatic, but it was tragic it happened the way it did.

Gaga: That kind of tragedy falls into the fixable category.

Me: I kind of agree. I've thought about calling her, but I'm not sure what to say because I don't think I did anything wrong. The problem is that Sophie thinks I did.

Gaga: You know what I'd say about that.

Me: Standing on ceremony is for fools?

Gaga: Bingo!

Me: No one says "Bingo" anymore, Gaga.

Gaga: (laughing)

Me: Even though I'm mad at Sophie, I miss her.

Gaga: I have no doubt she misses you too.

Me: So you think I should call her?

Gaga: You're so smart, April. I don't know why you're bothering to ask me the question when you already know the answer.

Me: Thanks.

Gaga: I'm always happy to help.

Me: Gaga, there's one more thing.

Gaga: Is it serious?

April: Very. I miss you.

Gaga: I miss you too, April.

*Reader, nothing is sweeter in this
sad world than the sound of someone
you love calling your name.*

—*Kate DiCamillo*, The Tale of Despereaux

Wednesday, May 27, 5:32 p.m.
Back from Brynn's

When I left the cemetery, I decided to go
to Brynn's house. Even though she hadn't
apologized to me, I wanted to tell her I
thought it was nice she'd told Sophie she was
sorry for the way she treated her.

When she opened the door, I didn't even
bother with a greeting. "I heard you apologized
to Sophie." Brynn slowly nodded. "That was
cool." I gave her a thumbs-up.

Brynn came outside and sat down on her

front steps and I sat next to her. "It doesn't really change anything," she said.

"I know. But it made Sophie feel better." I paused.

"What?" asked Brynn, like she knew I was about to say something.

I shrugged. I didn't really want to say what I was thinking.

"Are you wondering why I apologized to her?" asked Brynn.

"That's not it." I debated saying more. I knew Brynn was going to get mad, but it was now or never. "What I don't get is why you didn't apologize to me."

Brynn shifted like she was uncomfortable sitting on the brick front porch. "Why am I the bad guy? You did things wrong too."

"Yeah, I know," I said. "And then I apologized for it." I blew a hair off my face and stood. I don't know why I'd bothered coming. I guess part of me hoped Brynn would apologize to me too. I could see that wasn't going to happen.

I started to walk toward the street. "Wait."

Brynn followed me to the sidewalk. "I'm sorry," she said when she caught up to me.

She stayed quiet for a long time, and I didn't say anything either. The next move was hers. Finally, she spoke up. "This isn't easy for me. I've wanted to apologize to you. I've thought about doing it a bunch of times, but I didn't even know where to start."

I looked at Brynn, and her eyes were starting to tear up. But just knowing she was sorry wasn't enough. I had to know why. I sat silently, hoping she'd say more.

Brynn looked down and picked at a hole in her jeans. "I know I didn't handle things well last summer when Billy and I started going out at camp and I didn't tell you. I was scared you'd be mad. But I'm sorry. I wasn't being a good friend."

She inhaled like she needed air before she moved on to the next topic. "Then when Sophie moved here, I also wasn't nice to you. I guess I was jealous you had a new friend. I felt like I was being replaced."

She looked at me, and I could tell what she

was about to say next was hard. "And I'm sorry I blamed you when Billy broke up with me and started going out with Sophie. I know it wasn't your fault."

"Brynn, it's not that simple," I said.

Now it was her turn to be quiet while I talked. I reminded Brynn what happened when she came to my house the day after Thanksgiving and accused me of causing the breakup with Billy. "You yelled so loud that everyone in my house heard you say our friendship was over. And when we were at the diner on New Year's Day, you lashed out at Sophie, Billy, and me." I looked at Brynn. "You told me you hated me."

Brynn's face was ghost-white. "April, I'm really sorry." She paused. "For everything."

Then Brynn started crying. "I would understand if you don't forgive me. I'm not trying to make excuses. I was just upset about the breakup with Billy and your friendship with Sophie." She wiped her eyes on the sleeve of her T-shirt. "Everything changed when she moved to Faraway."

"It didn't have to," I said.

Brynn nodded. "I see that now. But I . . . I guess I just didn't know how to deal with it when it was happening."

"I get that," I said. But there was one last thing I needed to say. "Why didn't you come to Gaga's funeral?" I hadn't planned to bring it up, but this was my chance to get all of the things that were bothering me off my chest.

"I'm so sorry," said Brynn. "My parents wanted me to go, and I wanted to go. But after everything, I figured you wouldn't want me there."

"I wanted you there," I said. Then I paused. "Gaga would have wanted you there too. She loved you." It was true.

When I said that, Brynn really started crying. "April, this might sound crazy. But can we just start over? I'm so sorry about everything that happened." She wiped her eyes. "Could we try a fresh start? Please?"

I didn't have to think about it. After I broke my leg on the ski trip, Gaga gave me a speech about the healing power of forgiveness. I knew what she'd want me to do, what I needed to do. "I'd like that," I said.

She looked surprised, like she hadn't expected I would be so understanding. Before I could say another word, she reached over and gave me a big hug. "Thanks, April." Then she got a look on her face I knew well—it meant that Brynn was formulating an idea.

"Uh-oh. What is it?" I asked.

Brynn stood straighter. "We should go back to camp."

"Huh?" No part of what she'd said made sense to me.

Brynn continued. "I can ask my mom to call the camp and see if there's still room for both of us if we want to go. But it's a package deal. I'm only going if you go." She paused. "I'd really like to try to be friends again, and camp is the perfect place to do it."

My mind was reeling. I had already decided I wasn't going back to camp. In my mind, it wasn't even a possibility. But until recently, neither was the fact that Leo would be going to Costa Rica, or that Brynn and I might have a chance at being friends again.

Still, I had plans to be here this summer and work at Mom's store, and I was signed up to take a Driver's Ed class that starts next week.

I told Brynn about my job and the class. "I can't go," I said.

Brynn shook her head like neither of those things should prevent me from going. "You could reschedule the class and talk to your mom about working at the store when you get back from camp!"

"Wow," I said, mostly because I wasn't sure what else to say, but also because I was reminded that some things never change, like Brynn's ability to come up with a solution for pretty much anything—especially if it's something she wants to see happen.

Brynn bit her lip. "Can I try that again?" she asked, like she was aware of how she'd sounded.

When I nodded she continued. "I'd really like for us both to go to camp, but I get that you already have plans. So maybe if you could just think about it, that would be cool." She raised a brow. "Better?" she asked.

I had to laugh. "Much."

8:05 p.m.
Called Leo

I've been thinking about apologies since I left Brynn's, and I realized there's someone I owe one to—Leo. I haven't spoken to him or answered any of his texts since he told me two days ago he's going to Costa Rica. To be fair, it wasn't like I had this sudden realization I needed to apologize. I knew I did.

So tonight I called Leo and I got right to the point.

"I'm sorry I haven't called or texted you back. And I'm sorry I wasn't excited for you when you told me about doing research in the lab in Costa Rica." I paused. "I should have been, but it threw me for a loop when you told me you're leaving."

"April, there are three possible meanings of the expression *threw me for a loop*," said Leo.

"It's a reference to boxing, cattle roping, or riding on a roller coaster."

I laughed. "I know what you're doing. You don't want me to feel bad. But I do."

"To be honest, I'm flattered you like me enough to be upset I'm leaving. I was only upset that you were upset." It was such a sweet, Leo-ish way of looking at things.

"I'm going to miss you," I said.

"I'll miss you too," said Leo. "But the good news is that when I get back, we'll still have six weeks to spend together before I go back to school."

"Are we going to spend all that time talking about monkey brains?"

Leo laughed. "Even better. I'll show you pictures of them."

"Ewww!" I couldn't help but laugh.

"Actually, when I come back from Costa Rica, I'm starting a new research project," he said.

I groaned. "Isn't one per summer enough?"

"This one is of a more personal nature," said Leo. "I am planning to learn as much as I can about you, April Sinclair."

I wasn't sure if his line was a setup, but I took it as one. "There are a lot of things you don't know about me," I said in my most flirtatious voice. I thought it was a pretty good line, but I liked Leo's return even more.

"It sounds like the most fun research I'll be doing all summer."

9:10 p.m.
One more call

When I hung up with Leo, I knew there was one more call I needed to make.

I hadn't spoken to Sophie since the day she left. I still can't believe we spent a year being best friends and not having one fight, and the day she left, we ended our time together by having a fight in front of my whole family. Now that I've had a few days to think about it, all the things we said to each other seem so stupid. I wanted to set the record straight, so I called her.

But as soon as she picked up, Sophie beat me to it. "April, we're boneheads."

The way she said it made me laugh.

"Agreed," I said. "I'm sorry I didn't tell you about Billy."

"No, it's OK. You weren't the one who should've told me."

I had to agree with that.

"The day you left, I called Billy when I got home from the diner. I was so mad at him. I told him he should have told you sooner. He felt bad about the way it happened," I said. "He knew you were upset about leaving, and he didn't want to make you feel worse."

"It's fine," said Sophie. "I should have known it wasn't going to happen. I think I just wanted to believe there was something from Faraway I could take with me." She paused like she was trying to decide what she wanted to say. "April, I'm really sorry. Maybe I was jealous your summer was working out and mine wasn't."

Suddenly I realized there was something she didn't know. "Well, my summer isn't exactly working out the way I'd thought." I told Sophie about Leo going to Costa Rica and about Brynn apologizing and asking if I wanted to go back to camp.

"Wow!" said Sophie. "I leave town and the drama starts."

I laughed. "Something like that."

"What are you going to do?" asked Sophie.

"I don't know," I told her truthfully.

That's why love stories don't have endings! They don't have endings because love doesn't end.

—*Richard Bach*, The Bridge Across Forever: A True Love Story

Friday, May 29, 5:45 p.m.
Going to walk Gilligan

I still haven't decided what to do about going back to camp. Ever since I talked to Brynn, her proposal has been the main thing on my mind.

I'm torn. Part of me would like to go back to camp, especially since Leo will be gone, but part of me is having a hard time believing it's a good idea. Brynn and I spent the last five months not speaking. It seems weird to think everything that happened will be forgotten and we'll pick up where we left off. Or maybe we'll start something new. But there's still the issue of Brynn, Billy, and me all being together. I'm just not sure how that's going to work. And Mom is counting on me to help her at the store.

Brynn has been texting me all day asking if I have an answer. I'm going to walk Gilligan, and hopefully I'll find one.

6:12 p.m.

I found the answer I was looking for.

I didn't find it right away. I actually walked so far, I had to carry Gilligan home the last few blocks after he tried to lie down for a nap on the sidewalk. But as I turned the corner to my street with my dog in my arms, I figured out how I want to handle things.

There are two conversations I need to have. The first one is with Mom. I think she'll understand what I want to do, so that conversation shouldn't be too hard.

The second one is going to be a whole lot harder.

This morning, I texted Brynn and Billy to see if they wanted to go on a bike ride. What I didn't do was tell either of them that the other person was coming. I just said I had a surprise and to meet me at Mr. Agee's farm where we always stop for snacks.

Billy was the first to get there, but Brynn wasn't far behind. As she pedaled up to meet us, she looked suspicious.

And so did Billy. "What's going on?" he asked as Brynn got nearer.

It was a fair question. Billy and Brynn hadn't spoken to each other since January, and I hadn't told Billy about Brynn's apology. When Brynn got to where we were, they both looked at me like I had some explaining to do.

I motioned to the fence where we always sit and talk. "It's time for some honesty," I said once everyone was situated.

I looked at Billy. "Brynn and I talked. We kind of made up." Brynn and I smiled at each other. "Actually, we did make up," I added.

"Wow!" said Billy.

"Brynn wants us to go back to camp," I told him.

"Huh?" Billy looked shocked by what I'd said.

"Brynn's mom called the camp, and there's room for both of us to go." I looked at Brynn. "I want to go," I said.

"You do?" asked Brynn. I think if she hadn't been sitting on a rickety old fence she would have hugged me.

I held up my hand like I wasn't done talking. "But there's a condition. I only want to go to camp if all three of us are friends."

Billy and Brynn looked uncomfortable as I kept talking. "I think the problems between the three of us started when Billy and I started going out. Then they got a lot worse when we broke up and you two started going out."

"I'm the common denominator," Billy said. It was easy to see he was embarrassed by his role in the demise of our friendship. "I know it was messed up that I went out with both of you." He looked down and picked at a piece of rotting wood. "Sorry about that," he said.

Brynn nodded like she accepted his apology, and looked at Billy as she spoke. "I'm sorry too. I was pretty upset when we broke up."

She stopped talking, and her gaze shifted to me. She looked like she wasn't sure what else to say to Billy, and I couldn't blame her. Who wants to be stuck on a fence talking to a boy about how you felt when he broke up with you?

If Brynn and I were going to be friends again, now was a good time to start.

"The past is history. The future is a mystery. All we have is the present," I said. I knew I sounded ridiculous, but Billy and Brynn both laughed.

"You sound like one of your quotes," said Billy. He'd spent plenty of time over the years looking through the box in my room where I kept my collection of sayings that I liked, and this one was one of my favorites.

"We can't change what happened, but we should try to make a fresh start. I think camp would be the perfect place to do it, but we have to have a friends-only rule." My voice was all business, which I guess is why Billy started laughing.

"I've already learned my lesson the hard way," he said. "It won't be a problem."

Brynn nodded. "I agree completely. But I think there's something we're forgetting." She looked at me. "Did you talk to your mom?"

"Check," I said.

"Reschedule Driver's Ed?"

"Check to that too."

Brynn grinned. "You're going back to camp! It's official!"

"Almost," I said. I hopped down off the fence and opened my backpack. Brynn had always been the one that brought snacks, but today, I had come prepared. I brought out popcorn, mini Reese's, and lemonade— our snacks of choice since we became friends in third grade. I filled paper cups with lemonade and handed them to Brynn and Billy.

"Camp Silver Shores, here we come," I said as we clinked our cups together.

11:15 p.m.
In bed
Feeling proud
And happy

I feel really good about today. In the past, whenever Brynn, Billy, and I have had an issue, Billy was always the diplomat. But today, I'm proud to say I played that role. It was pretty obvious we all want to rekindle our friendship. Everyone knows we can't push the redo button or be the Three Musketeers the way we used to be. We'll be something different, but hopefully good.

One thing is for sure: we're going to figure it out this summer.

Sunday, May 31, 10:44 p.m.
Leo's last night in Faraway

Leo leaves for Costa Rica in the morning, so tonight, we hung out. We went to the mall, ate Middle Eastern food, and talked for a long time about the summer ahead. We're both excited about what we'll be doing. When we got back to my house, I was ready to say good-bye, but Leo had a surprise for me.

He reached into the mailbox, pulled out a small paper bag, and handed it to me. "Look inside," he said.

"Does it bite?" I asked teasingly as I slowly opened the bag and pulled out a box of stationery.

"You can write letters to me while I'm gone," said Leo.

I frowned. Leo is usually so thoughtful. "Isn't this kind of a selfish gift?"

"Nope," he said. "It's not selfish at all since I bought an identical box for myself." Leo grinned. "April Elizabeth Sinclair, will you be my pen pal?"

I bit my lip. The way he asked was so cute and sweet. "I'd love to be your pen pal."

Then Leo leaned over and gave me a long kiss good-bye. "It will be fun to be pen pals," said Leo when we were done. "But not nearly as much fun as when we're both back home and get to spend the rest of the summer together."

"Agreed," I said as I reached up and kissed him again.

When Leo left, I wasn't sure what to do with myself, so I did something I hadn't done in a long time. I called Brynn.

At first, Brynn was pretty quiet. It had been so long since we'd had a normal conversation, I thought maybe she was worried about saying the wrong thing.

"April," she said, then hesitated. I wondered if she was going to thank me for calling (which would have been weird) or get emotional (which would have been even weirder). But she didn't do either. "Do you want to go to the mall tomorrow and get stuff for camp?" she asked.

"Sure," I said. I had to give Brynn credit for knowing me well. It was exactly what I wanted to do.

Thursday, June 4, 9:32 p.m.
Happy birthday, June!

Tonight my whole family went to the diner to celebrate June's birthday. It was the first dinner we've all had together since Sophie and Emma left, and it made me miss them and Gaga more than ever. Especially after dinner, when we went around the table and everyone made birthday toasts to June. I kept thinking about what Gaga would have said and how much Sophie would have loved being there.

Even though I was sad as I thought about them, I was excited too. I knew June would love what I had to say.

"June, I have two presents for you," I said when it was my turn. The first one I got at the mall with Brynn. When we saw it, we both knew it would be perfect for my little sister.

"I love it!" June said as she ripped open the I LUV CAMP T-shirt I'd wrapped in blue tissue paper. When she was done, I gave her the other gift I'd wrapped this afternoon. "Open this one carefully."

"It's water in a jar," said June when she peeled the paper away. She looked confused.

"Do you know what kind of water it is?" I asked.

"I do!" screamed May. She'd seen that jar in my room plenty of times and she knew exactly what it was—the lake water Billy had brought home from camp for me the summer I didn't get to go.

I couldn't help but smile as I explained to June what she was looking at. "It's Silver Shores lake water, and I'm giving it to you because I don't need it anymore. Since I'll be at camp this summer, I can get all the lake water I want."

It didn't take June more than a few seconds to comprehend what I was saying.

"You're going to camp!" she screamed.

"Yep!" I nodded. I smiled at Mom and Dad. They'd made good on their promise to keep my secret so I could tell June on her birthday.

Even though it wasn't May's birthday, she looked just as happy as June. They both flew out of their chairs and gave me a huge hug. "I'm ecstatic!" said June.

"That's a big word," I said as she clung tight to me.

"I'm excited too!" said May.

I wasn't sure if she was saying it because she wanted us to know she was excited, or because she wanted to make sure anyone who was listening knew she understood the meaning of the word *ecstatic*.

Either way, I think it describes how we all feel. My sisters can't wait to go to camp and neither can I.

You have brains in your head.

You have feet in your shoes.

You can steer yourself any

direction you choose.

—*Dr. Seuss*

Friday, June 12, 8:47 p.m.
In the tub
Wearing Gaga's ski cap

Most people don't take a bubble bath wearing a wool ski cap. But they should. It makes for a decent shower cap when your dog ate your real one. Plus, it's extra warm and cozy, which makes for a very nice last bath before camp.

All I wanted to do tonight was soak in bubbles and think happy thoughts, which was exactly what I was doing when I was interrupted.

"Hey April, I need you." It was May knocking on the door. "I found a pile of T-shirts we forgot to iron name labels into. Can you help me?"

"I'm in the tub. Get Mom, Dad, or June to help."

"Please," said May. "Mom and Dad are busy and June is bad at ironing."

"No, I'm not," I heard June say.

Then there was a second knock on the door. "April, Mom says you have to get out NOW!" June overemphasized the word *now*. "It's my turn and she wants you to help May iron name labels into her shirts."

"Can't a girl take a bath in peace?" I yelled through the door at both of my sisters. I sank deeper into the water and pulled my ski cap down over my ears. It didn't totally block out the noise of my sisters continuing to bang on the door and telling me to get out, but it helped. Then my phone rang.

It was Brynn. I used a dry finger to answer it on speakerphone. "Can you help me decide which bathing suits to bring to camp?" she asked. I listened as she described the contents of her top dresser drawer.

"April, get out!" screamed May and June in unison.

"Just a minute!" I screamed back.

"What?" asked Brynn.

"Sorry," I said. "I was talking to May and June." I refocused my attention on the question she'd asked me. "I'd go with the red bikini, the yellow one with the flowers, and the purple one-piece."

"Good choices," said Brynn.

As soon as we hung up, my phone rang again and it was Billy. "Be at the bus stop by 6:15 a.m. so we get good seats," he said when I answered.

"I'll be there," I said. I was just about to tell him what snacks I was bringing for the ride to camp, when the lock on the door started to jiggle. I told Billy I'd have to call him back. "What's going on?" I screamed.

"I just read online how to pick a lock and I'm doing it," said June. As the door rattled and shook, it was pretty obvious she meant business.

"OK! I'm getting out," I said as I let the water out of the tub and grabbed a towel. Even though I'd wanted nothing more tonight than to relax in the tub, I was surprisingly cool with all the interruptions and door-banging.

In a way, all the chaos made me realize how excited I am about the summer.

I'm actually looking forward to having my sisters at camp. We've spent the last few days getting ready, and it's been fun being the expert talking with them about what's in store for the summer.

I'm excited to be going back with Billy and Brynn too. After the way things ended last summer, I never thought I'd be saying that. But tonight when Brynn and Billy called, it almost seemed like there never was a time when the three of us weren't friends. And that made me happy.

I know Gaga would be thrilled to hear me say that. She was all about happiness.

In a way, going to camp feels like yet another ending to add to this year. It's weird to know it's the end of my summers there.

But it's also a beginning—hopefully a new start to being friends with Billy and Brynn. And when we come back, I, April Elizabeth Sinclair, will be a sophomore in high school. It's kind of hard to believe.

But I'll deal with that when it happens. First: in T minus nine hours, I'll be on a bus on my way to camp with my sisters, with some of my best friends next to me and my favorite ski cap on my head.

What else could a girl need?

Ten Reasons My Life Is Mostly Miserable

1. My mom: Flora.

2. My dad: Rex.

3. My little sister: May.

4. My baby sister: June.

5. My dog: Gilligan.

6. My town: Faraway, Alabama.

7. My nose: too big.

8. My butt: too small.

9. My boobs: uneven.

10. My mouth. Especially when it is talking to cute boys.

THE MOSTLY MISERABLE LIFE OF APRIL SINCLAIR

Can You Say Catastrophe?

LAURIE FRIEDMAN

Too Good to Be True

LAURIE FRIEDMAN

Truth and Kisses

LAURIE FRIEDMAN

Not What I Expected

LAURIE FRIEDMAN

Too Much Drama

LAURIE FRIEDMAN

Love or Something Like It

LAURIE FRIEDMAN

A Twist of Fate

LAURIE FRIEDMAN

Life, Loss, and Lemonade

LAURIE FRIEDMAN

Acknowledgments

As Hillary Clinton and countless others have said, it takes a village to raise a child. Well, it takes a city to publish a book, and even more to publish a series of eight books. The Mostly Miserable Life of April Sinclair was written with the help of so many people.

First and foremost, I want to thank my amazing editor, Anna Cavallo, for helping April (and me!) see the light and always put our best foot forward. And to the extended team at Lerner—editorial, art direction, sales, and marketing—thanks for all your support and dedication.

I also want to thank my agent, Susan Cohen of PearlCo Literary. Thanks for all you do!

Thanks to my loving, crazy, opinionated, funny Southern family—my parents, sisters, grandparents, aunts, uncles, cousins, nieces, and nephew—for a lifetime of love, laughter, tears, and memories.

And of course, my most eternal thanks to my children, Becca and Adam, and to the love of my life, Albert. I love you all with all my heart.

About the Author

LAURIE FRIEDMAN has a lot in common with April Sinclair. She grew up in a small Southern town and had two younger sisters, a mother who owned a store, a father who liked to give advice, and the funniest, sweetest, wisest grandmother on the planet. Ms. Friedman collected quotes, loved to dance, and adored summer camp. She only wishes she'd had a boyfriend like Leo and a friend like Sophie. While writing the last April Sinclair book has been bittersweet, Ms. Friedman looks forward to creating new characters and books for kids of all ages.

Ms. Friedman is also the author of the popular Mallory series and many picture books. She lives in Miami, Florida, with her family and adorable rescue dog, Riley.